MILES AWAY FROM YOU

by a. b. rutledge

HOUGHTON MIFFLIN HARCOURT

BOSTON   NEW YORK

www.hmhco.com

The text was set in Bembo.

Library of Congress Cataloging-in-
Publication Data
Names: Rutledge, A. B., author.
Title: Miles away from you /
by A.B. Rutledge.
Description: Boston ; New York :
Houghton Mifflin Harcourt, [2018] |
Summary: Eighteen months after Vivian,
his beloved transgender girlfriend,
slipped into a coma after a suicide
attempt, eighteen-year-old Miles begins
healing while photographing her empty
shoes against the stark landscapes of
Iceland. Told through a series of instant
messages.
Identifiers: LCCN 2017003826 |
ISBN 9781328852335
Subjects: | CYAC: Love—Fiction. |
Coma—Fiction. | Bisexuality—Fiction. |
Transgender people—Fiction. | Conformity—
Fiction. | Suicide—Fiction. | Lesbian mothers—
Fiction.Classification: LCC PZ7.1.R92 Mil 2018 |
DDC [Fic]—dc23
LC record available at
https://lccn.loc.gov/2017003826

Manufactured in the United States of America
DOC 10 9 8 7 6 5 4 3 2 1
4500697316

For Alana Saltz

chapter one

Miles Away to Vivian Girl

April 25 8:49 PM

This will be my last message to you. I don't know why I'm still doing this, since I'm basically just talking to myself anyway. I guess I feel like I need to get my story straight. I need to put it all down so that tomorrow I'll be able to articulately say why exactly I'm dropping out of the case.

And that is, well . . . it's obvious that we're not going to win. I'm not your husband. We only dated for a year and a half. I have no legal rights to you.

And I know, okay, I know that this whole thing goes beyond win or lose. I know it's a statement. I'm taking a stand for your rights, and the rights of a lot of other people. But, damn, Vivian. I have rights, too. I CANNOT DO THIS ANYMORE.

I am not being articulate tonight. Just angry. I need to walk away.

Miles Away to Vivian Girl

April 25 8:53 PM

Why the fuck did you take all those pills, babe?

Miles Away to Vivian Girl

April 25 9:03 PM

So selfish. There. I said it.

Miles Away to Vivian Girl

April 25 9:13 PM

I'm done. I have nothing left to say to you.

Miles Away to Vivian Girl

April 29 12:14 AM

Okay, I know I said I was done, but here I am writing to you again because somehow—despite the coma—you just woke me up. My phone went off at midnight reminding me that it's the anniversary of the day we first started talking online. It had to be you that set the alarm a long time ago. I even got a new phone last summer. Stupid Cloud must have transferred it over.

My heart is racing. I didn't even know you had the capability to do that to me anymore. Five years, Vivian. Has it really been that long?

I remember how happy I was when you found me on DeviantArt and asked if you could use my scribbly cartoon explaining different gender identities in your online magazine. I was thirteen and convinced I'd been "discovered" as a fancy-pants artist. Even after I learned that you were only a couple years older than me and *Mixtape Mag* wasn't that big of a deal (well, not at the time, anyway), I still felt like this was something BIG AND IMPORTANT. And I was right. I can't believe how much *Mixtape*'s grown over the years.

I feel horrible about this: your website is gone. Everything. At first I tried to keep it running, but you're the one who set it all up. Nothing's in my name. Your parents sent me a cease and desist almost a year ago. And of course they didn't bother renewing the domain, so now everything's lost. Or it will be soon. I contacted the host, and there's a forty-five-day grace period, but there's no way the case will make it to court on time. What is even the point anymore? I can't save you. I can't save *Mixtape*.

I'm sorry.

I'm out.

Miles Away to Vivian Girl

May 1 6:15 AM

It's been a crap couple of days, no reprieve in sight. Especially after what I just did. I called my lawyer and told him he should go ahead and send the emails to your parents and mine, telling them I'm done with all this lawsuit bullshit. They can keep fighting if they want, but I can't anymore. I thought about it all night. I haven't slept. I wandered over to Brian's house at, like, four a.m., but I couldn't get him to wake up, so I'm sitting alone in the bed of his truck. I just saw the sun rise.

A minute ago, there was this plane. A little lemon-colored crop-duster on its way from the airport to spray pesticides on the field. I imagined for a moment that it was one of those sky-writer planes. I pictured it loop-de-looping as it etched out my deepest, darkest secret in fluffy white clouds for all the world to see.

I want my girlfriend to die.

I'm an atheist, a pacifist, a vegetarian, and a clingy, pansexual queer. Up until a year ago, a death wish was something I'd never experienced before. I'm the kind of guy who shoos insects out of the house by scooping them up on scraps of junk mail and ushering them out the front door.

I once rehydrated a slug.

And, yet, here I am. Wishing with all my might that you, an actual human being, would just quit fucking being alive. I'm the selfish one now. But I'm just so tired. Your parents want to pretend the real you never existed, and my parents seem to think that I'm the one who should get to call all the shots. I turned eighteen last month, and you know what I got? My moms marched me over to the courthouse and made me file a lawsuit. They called it a declaration of war. And for what? To give me the power to do what your family won't: pull the plug.

I've spent the last year and a half with all this anger. A hatred directed toward your parents who, despite all scientific and ethical reasoning, have elected to keep you on life support.

Normally, I seethe. I think about how your family members still call you by your birth name. How, after you were defenseless, they cut off your hormones and your beautiful hair.

And underneath it all, normally, there is pity. For the girl I love, who hated her body so much. I don't know what you were feeling that day. I wish you'd left a note. All I know is that you swallowed a bottle of pills and a bottle of vodka and then all the best parts of you blinked out.

You hated your body so much. And now your body is all that is left.

I've been waiting here for the cycle of negativity to come. I invited Anger and Pity and Seething and Rage to my one-man tailgate party, but I guess Apathy's the only one who's going to show up.

Soon your parents will check their email and cheer, having officially worn out the enemy before the battle even began. And soon my parents will check their email and know what a huge fucking disappointment I am.

And, two hours away from me, in a hospital just outside of St. Louis, a machine will keep you breathing—indefinitely now—while a nurse clips your toenails.

Miles Away to Vivian Girl

May 1 9:54 AM

Well, my phone is blowing up. A lot of people want answers from me right now, and I don't know what to say to them. I think I'll turn this thing off and take the long way on my walk home. Let my moms and all the lawyers and reporters catch my voicemail for a while. Later, V.

Miles Away to Vivian Girl

May 7 5:23 AM

You know who I hate right now? Your sister. She texted me the other day to ask when your parents could come get your stuff, and she actually referred to you as her "sibling." Like she's trying to be all gender-neutral and PC about it. Too late, bitch. Too. Fucking. Late.

So, they came last night. Your mom and dad showed up with a van and a couple of people from their church. I was sitting out on the fence under the welcome sign at Camp waiting for them to arrive. They stayed in the van until a cop car showed up, then all of them walked over to me, police escort in tow.

The cop said my full name like a question, and I said yes and led them down to your cabin. Officer Lewis said I could supervise, make sure they didn't take anything that wasn't yours. I plunked down on the couch and said, "They can have what they want."

I meant it. I was supposed to have everything ready and

packed up for them, but it's sort of impossible to tell anymore what's mine and what's yours. Since you've been gone, I've been staying at Camp a lot. Sleeping there, even. I guess you could say I moved in.

The cop sat with me on the couch and played around on his phone.

"Miles?" your mom called from your bedroom in the loft. Your parents peeked down into the main room and did that thing they always do where your mom pretends to be a sweet person and your dad folds his arms across his chest and shoots thoughts of fiery-hot damnation into my soul. "Have you seen hi—the Bible?"

Gaaaaaaawd. There were so many, so damn many, answers to that question. *Yes, Mrs. Loftis, I have seen the Bible. I know, I know, it's NOT Adam and Steve.*

Bible? Oh, there's hardly anything left of that old thing. You see, every Sabbath, your daughter and I would tear out a page, burn it, then commit most unholy acts of fornication atop the smoldering pile of ash.

Be civil, Mamochka always tells me. Do not engage.

"Mm-hmm," I said, grabbing your Bible off the bookshelf and tossing it into one of the cardboard boxes they'd brought.

"Thank you," she said.

"Uh-huh."

They didn't take much. Just . . . I don't know, kid stuff. Old-you stuff. Pre-Vivian stuff. Photo albums and trinkets and shit. They took your childhood, V. They didn't take any of your real clothes, of course. But I think those assholes took some of mine. Like that stripy sweater you gave me. I guess to them it seems like something either of us would have worn. Your sister was here with them, just kind of crying. I felt like I'd been punched in the gut. When they're around, I always feel like I've been punched in the gut. How much more of you do they think they can take from me?

Miles Away to Vivian Girl

May 9 10:16 PM

I just binge-watched an entire season of *Orange Is the New Black* and logged on here to tell you about it. That doesn't seem healthy. I guess it could be worse. I could be one of those people who throws birthday parties for their cats.

I feel okay. Not okay. Numb. Which is better than Constant Pain. Numb Is the New Okay. So much shit has happened, though, so I'm not going to talk about some TV show. I should update you on what's going on in my life. The life that I am still living because I have yet to try that booze and Vicodin combo that seems to have worked so well for you.

Everyone is so pissed right now. Strangers even. My inbox is full of hate mail from all over, people telling me what a shit-bag I am for not standing up for you anymore. As if some random person in, like, New Zealand should have a say in what happens to your body.

My mothers keep saying they're not mad at me. They

keep calling to tell me that they still love me. I wish they would just admit how pissed they really are. Mamochka never will, of course. She's been checking on me, like, every fifteen minutes, like she's genuinely worried I might try to off myself.

She must have forgotten that I'm on the Camp email list. I just got a huge mass email about you and how "we as parents" must make suicide prevention a top priority. Did you know, Vivian, that suicide is the second leading cause of death among youths aged ten to twenty-four? And did you also know that a whopping 41 percent of transgender youths have attempted to take their own lives? And ohmygodcanyouimagine that I am 100 percent done with this shit?

Miles Away to Vivian Girl

May 11 8:52 PM

I'm a horrible best friend. I haven't talked to Brian in months. I went to his house today to see if he would help me move the rest of your stuff before Camp opens again, but I felt so bad about ignoring him for so long. I ended up just asking to borrow his truck. He handed over the keys, and I did all the moving by myself. It's probably for the best.

I hate the idea of moving back in with my moms. But I just can't live there anymore. Not in that little cabin where you and I used to spend all our time. It doesn't even feel like the same place now that so much of your stuff is gone. I really loved us being out on our own. I felt like a grownup. Most of the time. Sometimes I knew we were just playing house.

When I showed up at my parents' house, Mom was at work, but Mamochka was home. She was working on a quilt, knitted panels scattered all over the living room. She rose out of the mess and sprinted to meet me in the entryway.

"I don't want to talk about it right now," I said. "But can I move back in?"

"Why do you think you even have to ask?" She threw her arms around me, pressing her ear against my chest. I remember one time you said that she and I were the same, that whatever we're feeling, we wear it. You were probably right. I could tell —just feel it in the air—how happy she was to have me back home.

And it's not like I was angry when I moved out. Or that there was some huge fight. I just wanted some independence. Some space. And now all that space feels like the tip of a freshly extinguished match pressed against my skin. Sulfur, heat, and pain without any flames.

Mom came home with Chinese takeout, and I could tell by the way she was acting that she'd already gotten a he's-here-and-don't-badger-him text from her wife. She put the food and her car keys down, then threw an arm around my back.

"We love you, son. We're not mad, okay?" she said. For the millionth time.

I nodded. I wanted to believe her, but I knew she was pissed. She was the one who'd decided to fight for power of attorney over you. Who convinced me. The one who'd filed the lawsuit. And the one who has decided to keep it up, despite the fact that I dropped out. Her actions turned your situation into a media circus. She answered phone calls from reporters and even let them fly her out to New York so she could debate conservative newscasters live on cable TV. She lives for that bullshit.

And I am trying, really trying, to not be mad at her anymore. I don't know if all this is just her chance to soapbox about LGBT rights, or maybe this is her way of repairing the wrong of losing a patient-turned-family-member. All I know is that whatever all this shit is, it's not about me.

"I want to go to Amsterdam," I told them at dinner. Just to break the silence. To talk about other things.

"Amsterdam?" Mamochka asked. "You'll just get into trouble."

"No, see, that's the point. I won't get into trouble, because everything I could possibly want to do is already legal there." I doubt I actually would get high or pay a complete stranger for sex, but maybe I want the option?

Mamochka stuck out her lip, but didn't say anything. Across the table, Mom had her eyebrows raised. Sex work is the one thing upon which my über-liberal lesbian parents do not agree. Mom thinks people should do what they want with their bodies, and Mamochka says human beings are not to be bought and sold.

I thought maybe I wanted to see them fight. Deep down I knew it was something else. "Actually, I don't even care if it's Amsterdam or Bumfuck, Texas. I just can't be here in June, okay?"

Camp. I know I can't handle it. Especially since they decided to rename it. Mamochka's idea, of course. Camp Vivian. Privately I've considered it Camp Vivian for a while now, because that's where I fell in love with you.

And, I mean, Camp means everything to me. How cool is it that my moms combined their individual interest of crafting and counseling into something—besides me—that they both really love? But I can't deal with the campers right now. You adored those kids, and they idolized you. How the hell am I supposed to be a role model for two dozen LGBT teenagers? Am I supposed to act like everything's going to be just dandy for them when they grow up? How am I supposed to even look at them when they know I couldn't fight for you?

Last summer, we shut down because none of us could handle Camp without you there. This year, though, everyone is ready to go back. Everyone but me, that is.

I really need to get the hell out of here, V.

chapter two

Miles Away to Vivian Girl

May 14 7:30 PM

I went back to the cabin. I still had to box up the stuff I didn't get around to moving when I had Brian's truck and tidy up the place. There wasn't a whole lot left to pack. Books and baskets of patterned paper scraps, all your art journaling supplies. I just took that all down to the arts and crafts hall. Figured you wouldn't mind.

I had to scrape up all the wax from the million little votive candles you'd let melt all over the corner of the sink.

Peel all the magnetic poetry off the mini fridge.

Wipe your kisses off the bedroom mirror where you blotted your lipstick.

And then there was the art still hanging on the walls.

You'd think I'd be sentimental about all this, but by that point, I was exhausted and enraged. It was one of those days when I got all angry instead of super sad.

So I did something horrible. I didn't mean to. It was just a lapse in judgment. A lack of impulse control.

I completely decimated *Winged Embrace*.

You know I LOVED that painting. I remember it from the first time you showed me the concept in your sketchbook. You, a dark-skinned and Afro'd grown-up version of one of Henry Darger's butterfly-winged girls—a Blengin? Is that what they're called? In your sketch, the boy holding you was just some generic guy. Not me, because when you originally drew it, you didn't know me yet. I remember tracing my fingers over the boy's ram's horns, feeling the indentations where you'd pressed down hard to make them black. I wanted to be that boy for you. I just didn't know then the crown of horns you'd give me would be so heavy and dark.

Later, when you had taken the sketch and turned it into an enormous painting, I got to be the boy with you in his arms. Well, it's me, and it isn't. Wild dark hair and olive skin, yes, but I'm not really that much taller than you, and I'll never look that good without a shirt. I appreciate the sentiment, though. Really, I do.

So there it was in the empty bedroom today. I couldn't make sense of how I'd been able to sleep alone under it for months and months and months. It was too big to fit in my car, and I didn't want to bug Brian again for his truck. I took it down, and I MEANT to just take the frame apart, but I guess I had a temper tantrum instead.

There was a box cutter involved. Rage. Little confetti

shreds of canvas. Snapshot bits, my arm, your leg. Mosaicked butterfly wings.

I regretted it instantly.

Later, after I became the Camp Vivian Dumpster Patron of the Arts, I went into the bedroom and started packing all your dresses away.

I found that stripy sweater. Guess they didn't take it, after all.

I also found A FUCKING BOX FULL OF MONEY, VIVIAN.

Holy shit, V. Good thing your parents didn't dig too deep in the closet, huh? (Maybe they were afraid they'd find another one of their kids *rimshot*.) But, holy shit. This is a lot of money. Not enough for your surgeries, but still a lot.

Why the hell would you hide something like this from me?

Miles Away to Vivian Girl

May 15 5:49 PM

Your grandpa is amazing. Seriously. GMH. I guess I should admit now that I spied on you sometimes. I heard you once on the phone with him, asking for money to help with the rent. Obviously a lie, since my parents were letting you stay in one of the empty cabins for free, but I figured that you probably just wanted some new clothes or something. Until I found that shoebox, I had no idea that you'd pouty-faced thirteen thousand dollars from him. Jesus. But I know that's where it must have come from. So today I went to his house and tried to give the money back. And he wouldn't take it. He told me he didn't want the hospital to have it. Or your parents. He said I should donate it to the Camp because "those kids need to be loved." I just lost it, V. I cried all over the place. I haven't cried like that in a really long time.

Miles Away to Vivian Girl

Mom's lawyer told me not to take any chances with the money I found in your wardrobe. So, I taped the whole box up and mailed it to your parents, despite what your grandpa said. Done. I'm sure that'll help them keep that tube down your throat for a while longer. Fuck.

But then Jon—that's the lawyer—told Mom about the money. Yesterday Mom woke me up during one of my marathon sleeping sessions. I've been sleeping a lot lately, because what else am I going to do now that my life has become the stuff of TMZ headlines and Lifetime Original Movies? Enroll in GED classes? Find a job? Get harassed by the press?

"Miles, it's three o'clock in the afternoon."

You'd think if Mom has learned anything during the years since my puberty hit, it would be to knock. Luckily I wasn't up to anything salacious. But the look on her face still made me feel like I'd been caught in the act.

In the aftermath of my decision not to follow through with your court case, I'd also decided not to follow through with any standard rituals of human hygiene. Mom stood in the doorway, glaring at the mess. Half-unpacked boxes of books, piles of clothes, dirty plates. Amidst it all: the tattooed slob wrapped in semen-and-tear-encrusted sheets that she calls her son.

"Yeah." I wanted to say something sarcastic, but I figure the less I say to her, the better. I don't need Dr. Mom analyzing my every word. She can't do shit for me, and we both know it.

"I need you to help me with one of the cabins. Please."

I knew going in that it was just an excuse to lecture me, but what was I supposed to do? I always get stuck doing the grunt work, what with me being the manly man around here. But Mom and I did manage to get through, like, forty-five minutes without actually speaking to each other. I mean, besides things like "pass me that hammer."

But it didn't stay quiet forever.

"You're killing me, kid." We were sitting on the roof patching shingles when she started to worry that we were getting sunburnt. She grabbed the tube of sunscreen stashed in the bottom of her toolbox, and we began slathering it on.

"What'd I do?" I looked around at the tiles, trying to figure out if I'd hammered one on sideways or something.

"The roof is fine. Just . . . you need to talk to me, okay? Why didn't you say you disagreed with the lawsuit? Or if you didn't want to talk with me, you could have told your Mamochka."

"Ohhh."

"What?"

"Nothing." I went back to hammering, though I'm not entirely sure if there were actual nails involved. I just wanted to hit something. The roof probably was fine, but Mamochka, sneaky Mamochka, thought that since all her mother-birding wasn't working, perhaps Mom could manage to intimidate something out of me.

"Quit screwing around, Miles." Mom yanked the hammer away from me, and it flew out of her lotion-slick hands and into the window of the next cabin over. Glass shattered majestically. And, of course, Mom got all Mom-ish, all hawk-eyed and intense. I hopped up, ready to make my escape, all in the guise of having a mess to clean up. But she grabbed the sleeve of my Modern Lovers T-shirt and pulled me back down beside her.

"You two would have done it anyway." Instead of looking at her, I concentrated on the tiles in front of me. I scraped a fingertip along the edges where the scratchy shingles turned from brownish red to black. My hands looked foreign to me, dirty for the first time in a long while.

I wish it were paint.

"Maybe," she said. "Maybe at first. But we had no clue it was bothering you. I mean, you seemed ready. Fine with it, even. Every day, putting on your suit and doing all that preliminary court stuff, and all that paperwork. You didn't once say you didn't feel like it was the right thing to do."

"Because it is the right thing to do. I just couldn't go through with it in the end."

"It's not the right thing if it's hurting you," she said. "I swear, it's like you got the best of both of us, but in the worst ways. You've got my sense of duty and your Mamochka's big heart. You're such a damn good kid."

"I didn't finish high school." Sense of duty? Ha!

"You followed a dream, though," she said. "You didn't just smoke weed on the couch, or something."

Funny that all this shit had to happen before Mom would ever admit that blowing off high school to draw comics, design coloring book pages, and help my internet-famous girlfriend run a popular website actually turned out to be an okay decision. I got lucky. I mean, how often does a sixteen-year-old have a chance to be art director of an online magazine? At the time, I had every intention of finishing school and doing my thing, but it was a lot of work. I had to choose, and in the end I chose you. I thought everything would turn out all right. "Good to know you think my career choice is slightly better than a drug habit."

Of course, I've now been avoiding that "career choice" for the past year and a half. Lately I've been helping out at Mom's office, filing paperwork and whatnot. I honestly don't see things the way I used to, and nothing, nothing, is fodder for comics and quirky coloring pages these days. The world simply isn't a weird and whimsical place without you by my side.

"I know how much pain you're in. But you're not processing. You're shutting down."

"Can you please not talk to me about 'processing'? You're not MY psychologist, you know?" Even if she was, could she help me? No. She didn't help you, and I'm not sure I'll ever forgive her for it.

"No, I'm your mother. And I can see more than anyone that you are falling apart."

"I'm not falling apart." I wonder what she'd say if she found out I've been IM'ing you all this time.

"I'm dropping the lawsuit."

You know, I've been wanting to hear those words for a while now, but it didn't make me feel any better. My stupid heart just sank a little bit deeper into my rib cage. Even my unflappable, crusading mother has given up hope.

"Okay, whatever. You do what you think is best."

"And I want you to promise me you're going to make an effort to start having a little fun, all right?" She continued like I hadn't said anything. "Hang out with your buddies. I bet there'll be some good parties soon."

Yeah, like my dropout ass would be welcome at a graduation party hosted by those jerks from high school. Probably should have said that to her, but instead I decided to keep on being a dick. "So, I should get wasted and rape somebody like all those other kids who really know how to cut loose?"

"That is not funny. Look, what I'm saying is that right now you're at a really volatile place. You can either continue this downhill plummet, or you can work through it."

"In other words, 'hold it together, son'?"

"No, Miles. I'm not saying you have to hold it together. I'm telling you that you don't have to hold it at all."

So, that's something to think about. I guess.

Miles Away to Vivian Girl

May 20 9:32 AM

Turns out I'm not the only one in this house suffering through these long, sleepless nights. Earlier, I walked outside at four in the morning to find Mamochka on the sun porch. It's only May, and already it's hot and humid, sticky, even in the middle of the night.

"Hi, baby boy."

"What're you doing up?" I plopped down next to her on the porch swing.

"Do you know much about Iceland?"

"Mm. Iceland is green, and Greenland is icy, right?" I was that loopy sort of tired. "Is this part of your crossword puzzle?"

"No, look." She was playing some sort of word game on her tablet, but she closed that out and opened up her camera roll. She flicked through a few images. Clusters of houses with colorful rooftops, fields of purple flowers, ice cave. "Look how pretty."

Pretty isn't the word I'd use to describe the images, but I knew what she meant. The photos she'd chosen were stunning, intricate. Full of patterns and shapes. They were exactly the sort of images you and I might have illustrated for *Mixtape.*

"Iceland is green. And in the summertime, nearly twenty-four hours daylight. Would be good for taking photos." Mamochka leaned against me, resting her head on my shoulder. "You won't be happy unless you get back to work, my darling. Make something for her. And for you."

It's not that I don't want to make something. I do. I can feel it almost, like this unbearable pressure. It's in my spine and my arms, my anxious clutching hands. It's behind my eyes, in my brain. It keeps me from sleeping, then wears me down until sleeping is all I can do.

And, trust me, I am tired of being a sad sack of shit. Really, I am. I know I know I know that I'm miserable and wallowing. I'm really screwed up. And no pretty purple flowers are gonna fix that.

It's like the other day, when I found all that money. Thirteen thousand dollars stashed away in an old shoebox that nobody even knew about. I had this wild thought that I should just take it. You can't look at that much cash and not let your mind spin out. Like, *I could take this money and I could just . . . go somewhere, or do . . .* Something? Yeah, that's as far as those thoughts got me. Somewhere and something.

Because it doesn't matter how much money or distance or sunlight I get. All the best parts of me are still going to be chained to that hospital bed.

I said none of this to Mamochka. Just clicked the lock button, and the pixels vanished from her screen.

I went back to bed, and when I woke up a few minutes

ago, there was a little package on my pillow, right next to my face. It was wrapped in that brown butcher paper we decorated at Camp a couple years ago. We'd all carved potato stamps and printed our own gift wrap. This was your paper, little rainbows and clouds.

I carefully peeled off the wrapping, and the first thing I saw was a four-pack of SD cards, which made me immediately feel guilty because I haven't even touched the very fancy, very expensive camera my parents got me for Christmas. Underneath the memory cards was a blank book, one of those Moleskine sketchbooks with the thick, buttery pages that I really like.

And tucked into the sketchbook was a photo of me and you. We were wrapped up in each other, and I was grinning as you kissed my cheek. We were holding a copy of the anthology we'd put together, a real-life copy of the best articles, art, and tidbits from *Mixtape Mag*. Our book, hot off the press.

Damn it, Mothers. Right in the feels.

Underneath the photo was an airline voucher to Keflavik, Iceland, round trip. A Post-it note on top said *NONREFUNDABLE*. Mom's handwriting. Big, bold letters.

So, yeah. It looks like I'm going to Iceland. In, like, a week and a half.

chapter three

Miles Away to Vivian Girl

May 22 6:54 PM

Just so we're clear—because I wasn't even sure myself at first —my parents are sending me to Iceland alone. I was worried for a minute they'd decided to shut down Camp so we could have some happy-go-lucky family retreat. Camp is still on, my moms are still running the place, and I'm glad. I am a little nervous, though, about going somewhere so far away on my own.

I went to see Brian at the restaurant earlier. His parents pretty much have him managing the place now that he's graduated. It means he's busy a lot, but on the plus side, he did give me a shit-ton of free cheese fries.

"How was prom?"

"Kind of a bust. You think it's going to be a big deal, but then you get there and it's just another stupid high school dance," Brian said. "Terrible music. Lots of twerking. People crying."

"And graduation?"

"Terrible music. Lots of twerking. People crying."

"Ah, good," I said, and I found myself smiling for the first time in a while. "I was afraid I was missing out."

I told him about the trip. Figured he might want to come along.

"Iceland?"

"Yeah, man. Supposed to be really pretty right now. So, do you want to go? There's probably still time to get you a ticket."

"That's really cool, man. But, I can't. I gotta adult."

"No! You can't do this to me, Brian. Please don't do this to me. You can't adult."

"I know. I know. Trust me, nobody regrets this more than me. But, look." He waved his hand around, gesturing to his recently inherited kingdom of fry cooks and oil vats. "Someday all of this will be mine."

I groaned and speared a few more fries with my fork. "I never thought I'd say this, but I miss high school. No. Not that. What I really miss is being small enough to ride in the shopping cart at the grocery store. Those were the days."

He smiled and stretched his gigantic arms across the back of the booth. I bet Bri doesn't even remember riding in a shopping cart. His limbs were probably too long at age three. "No, man. You're gonna have a hell of a time in Iceland. You know what I've heard about that place?"

"Uh, that it's green and Greenland is icy?"

"Nah. I've heard it's super easy to get laid. There's even this website that gives you tips on how to get Icelandic girls to go home with you and stuff. I'll have to send you the link. Also, I saw this old interview with Quentin Tarantino where he said pretty much everyone there is really, really hot. Like, even the girls working at McDonald's. I wish I could go!"

"Yeah. But wouldn't Megan be pissed if you went off to screw some Nordic women with me?"

He sighed. "Man, Megan dumped me."

"What?" I said. "When?"

"Like three months ago, maybe. She met this guy at her fancy new bank job. I don't know."

"That sucks, man," I said. They'd been together since freshman year. "I'm sorry."

He shrugged.

"Why didn't you say something? Even though I've got all this shit going on, you know you can still talk to me, right?"

"Your phone can place outgoing calls, too, Miles."

Ouch.

After I left the restaurant, I had to run a few errands for Mamochka. When I got home, Brian had already sent me the link to the How to Hook Up with Icelandic Chicks website. And an 8tracks mix entitled "Music to Lay Your Lady (or Man or Whatever Miles Is Diggin' These Days) Down To." What a bro.

Miles Away to Vivian Girl

May 24 3:14 AM

I just had a panic attack. At least, I think so. I'm thinking about all those times I'd sit with you gasping beside me and all I could do was rub your back and tell you to breathe. Slow down, V. Slowly. Deep breaths. I don't have anybody to do that for me. Mamochka, maybe, but she's sleeping, and it'd just worry her more. And I'm too old for that shit, man.

And you wanna know what brought all of this on? This awful panic attack stuff? A fucking three-pack of Trojans.

Because, yes, I bought condoms for my trip. The smallest box I could find, and it still feels like a thousand-pound weight on my chest.

Miles Away to Vivian Girl

May 24 3:23 AM

And, God, I can't even say it. I can't even type it to a faceless oblivion. That's how ashamed I feel right now.

Miles Away to Vivian Girl

May 24 9:32 AM

Okay. I've slept a little. Not a peaceful drift, but pure exhaustion. I feel a little clearer now, though. So, we can try this again.

I want to have sex with someone.

First of all, I'd choose you. In a heartbeat. Like, if some

magical hookup fairy came to me and said, *You can bang anyone you want, Miles, anyone in the whole world. Hell, even aliens are up for grabs if you're into that freaky tentacle shit.* I'd be all, *No, ma'am, just Vivian please. Awake and alive and in my arms.* No question. BUT meanwhile in the real world . . . I am losing my mind here. I hate thinking this whole thing is about sex. Am I really that basic?

There's no guidebook for Comaland, though. Nothing to tell me that a year and a half is long enough. I wish YOU could tell me a year and a half was long enough. Just like I wish you'd been able to rub my back and tell me to breathe, but, no, I'm just feeling my way in the dark, and it really, really sucks.

Maybe a year and a half is too long? Maybe I'm a loser for waiting around when I know you're not going to wake up, and even if you did, you wouldn't be you and we'd still never ever sleep together again. Brian definitely thinks I've waited long enough. And so does his cousin Audrey, who tried to hook up with me, like, a year ago. I almost did. I mean, the pants were off. But then came the guilt.

Damn, I've got more hang-ups about sex these days than a Pentecostal preacher's daughter. I want to not feel guilty. I want to not feel like I'd be cheating on you. I can't have that, like I can't have one last little kiss on the shoulder. I'm not asking to fall in love again. Definitely not ready for that. But I'd like someone to touch me. And maybe push you to the back of my brain for a little while.

Miles Away to Vivian Girl

Just finished packing. I laid everything I needed to take to Iceland out on my bed like one of those knolling-style photographs you always see on travel blogs and menswear ads. A collection of related items, perfectly sorted and neatly arranged. There's something soothing about creating order from chaos. I folded my wrinkled jeans and worn-out boxer briefs. Belt, passport, iPad, tiny toiletries, guidebook, chargers. Other than a few dumb slogan tees and a handful of ¾-gauge earrings, it was all pretty run-of-the-mill stuff.

It's funny how boring it all seemed. Guess I'm pretty generic. On paper, anyway.

I unzipped my suitcase to find a slight dusting of white sand, a souvenir from my last big trip. The Definitely Not Disney Trip to Florida. You made us all swear up and down that we wouldn't set foot in the Magic Kingdom.

"Why on earth," Mom had asked, "don't you want to go to Disney World?"

"Because my parents haven't ever taken me," you said. "I just think it's something all parents HAVE to do."

You were sixteen. At that point it seemed highly unlikely that your parents would ever take you to Disney, especially if you weren't on speaking terms.

I was fourteen, and my parents had never taken me to Disney. And since you weren't my girlfriend at the time, just this new and constant fixture at my house, I had to point out the fact that you were ruining my chances of meeting Mickey Mouse — not that that was ever a life goal or anything. Now, Princess Jasmine . . . maybe.

So, anyway, we all went to Florida. We drove because you were afraid of getting x-rayed and felt up by the TSA agents. We stayed in a condo that looked like a Barbie Dream House, and you and I soaked in the enormous bathtub together with our bathing suits on. Instead of Disney World, we went to Universal Studios, which, honestly, I think is probably better anyway. Because: Harry Potter.

That was a good trip. A happy trip.

Sometimes when I get really angry about your parents, Mamochka tells me that they're just loving you the only way they know how. Like, somehow, keeping you alive makes up for being the reason you wanted to die. It never quite makes sense, but it used to be enough to calm me down. Now I think it's bullshit. It's bullshit, and I hate them for not loving you the right way and for never taking you to Disney World.

You should have let us take you instead.

Miles Away to Vivian Girl

June 1 12:55 AM

I'll be close to you tomorrow. The airport's only, like, thirty minutes from your hospital. But I can't go see you, because your parents filed an ex parte. Weird, isn't it? I'm the last person you'd ever think would get slapped with a restraining order. I wish I'd known the last time I saw you it was truly the last time. I don't know what I could have done differently, but there does seem to be a lack of closure here. So, for now, I'll have to browse through my photos of you and kiss my phone screen goodbye instead of your cheek. Not really. I don't actually make out with my phone or anything. That would be weird. I miss you, V. Love you.

chapter four

Miles Away to Vivian Girl

June 1 3:45 PM

Well, goddammit, I missed my flight. A connecting flight. There aren't any flights from St. Louis to Iceland, so I had to fly to Boston first, but for whatever bullshit reason, I had this tiny little layover in Charlotte. Forty-five minutes. What the hell kind of layover is that? And since my last flight took thirty-five extra minutes to get off the ground, that gave me, like, ten minutes to haul ass across this giant airport, but by the time I got to the gate, it was too late. They're putting me on the next flight to Boston, which arrives at eight. My flight to Keflavik leaves at nine, so assuming I can book it across another ginormous airport, I could still make it.

I'm exhausted. I've been up since the crack of dawn. First a two-hour drive to St. Louis, then this mess. I haven't eaten because I thought I'd eat in Boston while I was waiting for my flight, but it looks like I have to eat now or not at all until

I cross the Atlantic. So I bought a slice of pizza, but I'm too anxious to eat it. And now I'm annoyed at myself for wasting money.

The airport goodbyes in St. Louis were as teary and awkward as you'd expect, but now that I'm away from Mom and Mamochka, everything's starting to sink in. It's like I was bluffing this whole time. I didn't actually expect my parents to be okay with me leaving like this. Do you know (of course you don't) that I'm going to be there for a month? Seriously, they booked me an entire month at a hotel. How can we afford that? I'll be away the whole time Camp's going on. They must not want me near the place. I must be in really bad shape, V.

Miles Away to Vivian Girl
June 2 9:15 AM

This is literally the best sandwich I've ever eaten. It's got, like, sliced boiled eggs, tomatoes, romaine lettuce, and some sort of Thousand Islandish dressing on it. And you know how much I hate Thousand Island. But it is literally the best sandwich I've ever eaten because it's the first food I've had in twenty-four hours. And it's European. Yes, V, I made it to Iceland. I'm in a hotel lobby that is very modern and . . . dare I say "posh"? Yes, I think I will say posh because that would be the properly European thing to say. Anyway, this is definitely not a Motel 6.

Also, right next to me there's a statue of a sheep that

appears to be made from lumber scraps, and somehow it is very posh, too. I have named this sheep Sven, and he's guarding my suitcase while I stuff my face and try to type with one hand.

I would like to tell you about the flight and what little landscape I've seen, but I'm so exhausted and dizzy-headed that all I can think about is this sandwich and wooden sheep. I've had no food and no sleep for a full day now. All I want is a bed, an actual bed, but my room isn't ready. A scheduling error, the little guy at the front desk said. He is very sorry. His hair is up in a man-bun. His accent is amazing. I'm not even going to yell at him because I seem to be experiencing some sort of post-flight-delirium, and also I never yell at customer service reps because I know those kinds of jobs must suck. I'm sure it's not Man-Bun's fault they overbooked. Plus, he gave me this sandwich, and it's the fucking best. Right, Sven?

Miles Away to Vivian Girl
June 2 7:54 PM

Jet lag: the struggle is real. I've slept away most of my first day in Iceland. I didn't sleep at all on the flight. I had a window seat, and I just kept staring down into the ocean. I'm a Missouri boy, after all. It's hard for me to fathom how that much water even exists.

It was cold and rainy yesterday when we landed at the airport, which is tiny and made of glass. I went through customs and got a stamp from the second country I've ever visited (Canada being the first—but that hardly counts!), then stopped to take a stupid selfie under the WELCOME TO ICELAND sign for Mamochka and Mom.

After I got out of the airport, I had to wait on a bus to Reykjavik. The plane ride had really taken its toll. I was anxious from sitting too long, but too tired to do anything about it. I sat outside underneath an awning and just stared into the distance for a long while. There's a sculpture in the parking lot. It looks like a bird—or a dinosaur, maybe—hatching out of an egg. Just one unrecognizable limb thrust out into the world. The rest of whatever-it-is inside that shell probably hasn't made up its mind about whether or not it wants out.

That's when I let myself miss you. Not enough to get all weepy about it. Well, maybe I did tear up a little bit. What I'm trying to say is that I really wanted you there with me. And this whole trip was starting to seem like a really bad idea. I mean, who does this shit? I don't know a single person that's gone off to a foreign country for a month all by themselves at the drop of a hat. No planning. Here's your ticket. Boom.

What happens if I get sick? Or lost? What if I just need someone to hold my hand?

If you Google Iceland, you're bound to get blown away by all the beauty, but the bus ride was kind of underwhelming. Forty-five minutes of bumpy lava fields. Puke green and unreal, but not necessarily pretty. And in the distance, mountains like you've never seen before. Tiny. Like steep, pointed hills. They don't tower the way American mountains do. They just sit there, totally chill, watching your bus roll along. After fifteen minutes, it was old news and I was dying for the scenery to change, but it didn't until we hit the city. And Reykjavik doesn't even seem like a city. Two-lane traffic. Quiet and calm. The architecture doesn't strike me as European. Everything is a little rundown-looking, but all of this makes me feel more relieved than disappointed. It's not intimidating. I mean, I feel like I could get by okay here. I am especially grateful that everyone knows English.

The first bus took me to a bus station, and another bus took me to the hotel. The driver asked me which hotel, and I got embarrassed about whether or not I pronounced Skógur correctly. Who knows? But at least he didn't laugh. I'm sure Americans have butchered worse.

By this point, I was wearing pretty thin, really looking forward to crashing at the hotel. But, as you know, my room wasn't ready. I was so out of it I started to get the sensation that the floor was kind of wavering, all bumpy and rolling like the lava fields. Not good. The awesome sandwich did help flatten things out, but I was stuck waiting for about half an hour while they decided what they were going to do with me. Eventually, I did fall asleep, curled up in one of the lobby chairs.

The guy with the bun woke me up, tapping me on the knee. "Hey. Come with me." He had a huge laundry sack slung over his shoulder, but he insisted on carrying my suitcase, too. We got in the elevator and he pulled out a set of keys and showed me—twice, actually—how to insert one of the keys into the control panel. I was so tempted to go, *Aw, shucks, we don't have none of that fancy key technology back home!* Mamochka would be proud I managed to contain myself. He hit a button marked *P,* and up we went. I sometimes get a little claustrophobic in elevators, but I decided not to lose my shit about it around him. We got out in this blank gray landing with nothing in it but a tiny spiral staircase. Kind of creepy and industrial-looking. I followed him up the stairs, and just when I was starting to wonder if he was actually the kid from *Let the Right One In* luring me to a dark corner so he could drain my blood, he opened the door and all this sunlight streamed in.

Apparently *P* stands for whatever the Icelandic word for *roof* is.

"What do you think? Just for today and tonight? If it's not okay, I'll call around and find you a room at another hotel for the night. You have my sincerest apologies."

And I was like, "ARE YOU KIDDING? THIS IS GORGEOUS!" Because it was. Wedged in between shoulder-high brick walls, there was a little open-air "room" with this big round lounger thing and jungly potted plants and a bohemian-looking rug. A canvas canopy looped with Christmas lights provided shade from the sun, which had decided to come out during my little nap in the lobby. On the cement floor around the canopy, rain pooled into puddles here and there, reflecting little patches of cloudy sky. Gorgeous, V. Gorgeous. "Can I stay here the whole time?!"

"No bathroom," he said. "And it can get a bit chilly at night. It won't be too cold tonight, though. Around sixteen, I think."

"Sixteen? Degrees?" Crazy, invincible Nordic people!

"Celsius," he reminded me. "That is maybe . . . sixty for you."

"Oh. Right. That's not bad."

He overturned his laundry sack on the lounger. Inside was a set of bedding and some big, fluffy pillows . . . I started daydreaming about sleep again. I helped him try to make up the bed—impossible, really, to make rectangular sheets fit on a round bed. But we tried.

He smoothed out the comforter one last time, then stood up straight and started working the elevator key off his key ring. He also gave me a magnetic key card. Apparently, there's a spa downstairs with a restroom and showers and a huge, heated pool. It's closed after five, but he told me I could come and go as I pleased after hours as long as I didn't invite any of the other hotel guests along. He apologized a few thousand more times and finally left. I crashed, taking a blissful eight-hour nap under the warm, Icelandic sun.

Miles Away to Vivian Girl
June 2 11:22 PM
Why do I keep writing to you? I guess I still have things to say.

And I know that writing things out can help cement memories. For a long while now, I've been living in this black, colorless void. Bedroom. Kitchen. Cabin. Couch. Food. Sleep. Sleep. Sleep. I couldn't name one interesting thing that's happened in the past year. I'm starting to worry that the part of my brain that's supposed to hold on to stuff—good stuff, pretty stuff, whatever—might not be able to latch on to new things anymore. Mom says that can happen. Trauma can steal your memories. Like if a person is having a really hard time, sometimes their brain will just block out that whole time period a year or so down the road. She says Mamochka once told her she can't even remember her ex-husband's face. I don't think I'll ever forget yours.

I guess now's as good a time as any to tell you that I'm wearing your boots. Those Docs you had your heart so set on, and I hated that they were leather, but I bought them for your birthday anyway, cows be damned. Now I'm wearing them because you aren't and they might as well be put to good use.

I just got done chatting with Mamochka. The Camp kids have arrived, and everyone's in bed now. It's late, there and here. The sun didn't set until after eleven. I'm wide awake under the sparkly Christmas lights, Reykjavik twinkling back at me in the distance. The hotel's off in a vacant field, with no other buildings very close. I'm eating Icelandic potato chips, which aren't any different than American ones, but . . . Man, don't even get me started on this lousy excuse for Mountain Dew. It tastes like Mello Yello, so screw that. What am I going to do with myself? I don't even know what I'm going to do for tonight, like, entertainment-wise. I hear the nightlife in Reykjavik starts super late, so I could go wander around, but I'm not feeling up to the noise and lights of the bars yet . . . or the people. I'll get there. Just not tonight.

I wish I were more of a drinker. Or a better one. All it does is make me sad and sleepy. Remember when you tried to get me drunk for the first time? You had this great plan to get me shitfaced and make me fun, as if my first tequila sunrise would not only change my life, but yours as well. I told Mom and Mamochka I was staying over at Brian's, but I spent the night at Camp with you instead. You made me try a bunch of different mixed drinks, and I didn't like any of them.

"Quit photographing your booze and drink up!" I can still picture you sitting across from me in the empty Camp mess hall. Violet lipstick and that big yellow bow in your hair.

"But they're so pretty!" Okay, I did get a little drunk.

"I just don't understand how the two most amazing people on the planet raised this." You waved your hand all around my face. "You're like a blanket stuck in the mud."

"What? I think you mean either a wet blanket or a stick in the mud."

"No, it's a combination of both. You're just this sad, muddy security blanket that some kid tossed out the car window when he finally decided to be cool." Looking back, it seems like such a mean thing for you to say. But that's just kind of how we communicated. We teased each other a lot.

But that night I was a little too tipsy to get clever and catty with you. I just smiled. "Lucky you found me, huh? 'Cause I turned out all cute and snuggly once you got me home and cleaned me up."

I hope you know I always felt that way about you. Grateful. So fortunate. Even though it was my family that took you in when you had no place to go, I think it's safe to say that me, Mom, and Mamochka all thought it was the other way around, that we'd been adopted by you.

You moved from your side of the booth and slid in next to me. Colorful half-finished drinks dotted the tabletop, and your lips were on my throat. "I'll show you lucky. Let's get out of here."

We walked back to your cabin and fooled around a little bit, then you surprised me with a gift, for no reason at all. It was that big Sandman omnibus I'd been wanting. I squeed over it for a little bit, and you said, "You want to read it right now, don't you?"

"Uh-huh."

"I shouldn't have given it to you until the end of the night."

"That's what she said."

You laughed and kissed me, then you asked if you could drive my car. You hadn't had anything to drink, so I handed over my keys, and we went out to that cemetery you always liked. I remember we sat on the back bumper and kissed, but we didn't linger there too long. We hardly ever kissed in public like that. That's one thing I really regret. One thing I couldn't find a way to change or control. I never figured out how to make us feel safe.

You took the long way home, gravel roads. I brought the Sandman book along and had it open on my lap. The moon was full, and occasionally there'd be a break in the trees, just enough light on the pages for me to catch a glimpse of Desire and Delirium. You plugged your phone in and played a song for me. "Tonight and the Rest of My Life." I'll never forget it because it's the sort of song you only need to hear once. The lyrics just sink into your heart.

I rolled the window down. The air was so cold, and it ruffled the pages of my new book. When the song was over, you pulled onto some dark side road, and you had that little container of stuff to make glow-in-the-dark bubbles. We made a huge mess mixing the glow-stick stuff into the bubble solution. It was all over my pants and your hands. You smeared it on my cheeks like war paint. We got out of the car, some country road in the middle of the night, and blew radioactive bubbles in a tilled-up cotton field. It was fun. It was so fun. I think about that night a lot because it's the last time I remember things between us being really, really good.

Seems like after that day, winter hit hard. The royalty checks from the *Mixtape* anthologies started coming, and you could hardly believe that you were out on your own and getting enough money to pay the bills by doing stuff you loved. It seemed like a dream come true until your parents cut you off their insurance and the public health care system decided you were rich enough to afford your own damn meds.

Two days before Thanksgiving, you cracked one of your wisdom teeth. On a cheese quesadilla of all things. The dentist convinced you to go ahead and have all four of them pulled. On the way home from your surgery, I dropped off the prescription the dentist had given you for pain meds. I took you home, tucked you in, then headed back to the pharmacy in case you were in pain when you woke up.

"It shouldn't be so much. It's only Vicodin," I said when the pharmacy tech rang me up and an exorbitant amount of money flashed on the cash register screen.

The tech did some typing around and told me there was a second order, a monthly auto-fill. "It's been ready since last week."

"Uh, just the one from today. She'll pick up the other later." I didn't have enough cash to pay for both. Painkillers were the only thing on my mind at the time.

When I got back to the cabin, you were awake. Messy hair, tired eyes. Wearing a little strappy top and those plaid pajama pants you stole from me. You'd probably hate to hear this, but you looked really pretty. I liked the no-makeup Vivian as much, if not more, than when you were all dolled up. I plopped down beside you on the bed and asked if you were in any pain. You said no, but took one of the pills just in case. We missed the part where you're supposed to eat first, though, so it made you sick and dizzy. You put the rest of the bottle in the cupboard and said, "Never again."

When you were feeling better, I asked about the other prescription.

"It's nothing," you said. "Just a bottle of antiandrogens. I'll be fine without them for a few more weeks."

I took a moment to kiss your bare collarbones. Because they were there and I liked them. Because I forgot that you did not. They were a part of you that the hormones had yet to soften up. You tried to shake me off, but I just cuddled you a bit more. "You sure?"

"Yeah. It was them or Christmas presents—no, shhh! Don't argue with me. It's no big deal. Just don't be alarmed when I"—you dropped your voice all low and manly— "develop a sudden interest in football and kung-fu movies."

And I laughed a little because I could not have cared less if you butched up a bit. But it did kind of surprise me that you were okay with it.

It was only later that I started to notice that things with you weren't totally okay. After you decided to come out as trans on *Mixtape* and we watched our readership shift from cis teen girls to a new crowd, mostly LGBT.

After that day I came home to find you crying, and you said, "Real girls don't like me anymore." And I didn't think to correct you. You are a real girl.

After I found that overstuffed folder in your email marked *Haters*.

After the Christmas dinner where your parents didn't show.

After the fight where I told you that you should "just give up" (on your parents, Vivian — I swear to Christ I meant give up on your unsupportive asshole parents).

After I found you blue in the face.

After the doctors said the odds weren't looking so good.

That's when I went to the pharmacy and picked up that bag of meds you'd decided to skip that month, citing financial reasons. (Despite having thousands and thousands of dollars secretly hidden away — what the hell???)

And I found out they weren't antiandrogens or hormones.

You'd stopped taking your antidepressants.

chapter five

Miles Away to Vivian Girl

June 3 5:15 AM

According to the Internetz, *skógur* means "forest." And I believe it. I've just spent the last two hours exploring the hotel. The rest of it is just as pretty and atmospheric as the roof, and there is a neat enchanted forest kind of theme. Each floor has a different sort of tree for its motif. There are pines on the first floor and some kind of ancient-looking trees with gnarly roots on the second. I like the top floor the best—the walls in the hallways are made from rows of birch trees. I ran my hand over them, feeling the bump bump bump as I wandered through.

I felt a little weird skulking around in the middle of the night, so I took a towel and a bag of toiletries with me, figuring that if anybody wanted to know what I was up to, I'd say I was looking for the spa, even though Man-Bun told me it was on the first floor. Anyway, Mamochka was telling me earlier that this place has, like, a movie theater, a library, and a little art gallery. The gallery was locked, and I never did find the library. The theater was open and running. It must be 24/7. I walked in to see some Icelandic lava documentary playing on the screen and a young couple going at it in the third row. Well, shit. No documentary for me. I booked it out of there while they tried to unfuck themselves. Ha.

Finally I did go to the spa. Swipe, and I was in. I had to feel around for the light switch in each room. Found the pool easily, but didn't feel much like swimming. Since I had the whole place to myself, I—strictly for the hell of it, not because I have any gender issues—walked around in the women's shower room. Nothing interesting, though. I kept wandering through and eventually ended up in the men's showers. There were no individual stalls, just a big, open locker room kinda shower.

It's funny how masturbation has become such an autonomous thing to me, like I'm just hitting puberty all over again. I was alone and naked. My dick was, like, *Hey, while you're scrubbing your balls, you might as well . . .* and I was so busy mentally casting myself as "unnamed male fornicating in theater" that it took a minute to register the fact that I had started jerking it in a public shower where, theoretically, any employee possessing the right key card could have walked in on me.

My mind was flickering all over the place, thinking about you and people who aren't you and what it'd be like if someone did walk in on me. I almost wanted it to happen, like I needed someone to burst in and say, *Hey, you can't be in here enjoying yourself. Your girlfriend is in a coma, for Chrissake!*

Or, alternatively, *Hey there, stud. Need a hand with that?*

I don't know which one I wanted more.

But, anyway, yeah . . . I did, ahem, enjoy myself. In a public shower. Pretty gross, right? Well, at least now I can say I've achieved orgasm on two continents.

Miles Away to Vivian Girl

June 3 1:30 PM

I wouldn't exactly say I'm extroverted. Not like you were. I don't have a lot of friends, and it doesn't bother me. You were my whole world for a while. I feel kinda shitty for ditching Brian all the time when you and me first started dating. Anyway . . . where was I going with this?

Loneliness? Yeah. I was lonely this morning, but in a different way. Not a lonely-without-Vivian sort of way, but this big, overarching strange-man-in-a-strange-land sort of way. I woke up in time for breakfast and found out that hotel patrons don't just get a muffin and orange juice here. They get a free breakfast buffet. And you know how much I love breakfast foods! I was more excited than that rat in *Charlotte's Web* when he gets to munch on all that carnival food. What was his name? Templeton? I loaded up my plate with this random assortment of stuff that I wanted to try—beans on toast, little baby potatoes, soft-boiled eggs, lemon curd. *Skyr,* the famous Icelandic yogurt. Earl Grey tea. Stuff I haven't really had before. And that was when I got a little lonely because I didn't have anyone to share the experience with.

And then Man-Bun showed up. "I have some things for you. May I sit?"

He's very proper. His back is very straight. His hair is whitish-blond, and his eyes are very blue. We make each other nervous, because we're both extremely awkward people in extremely different ways. We need someone like you as a buffer. If you were there, you'd have grabbed his arm and said something weird and funny, probably your standard line about how black people don't bite—as if your skin color were the reason strangers were curious about you. Anyway, you weren't there, so I was stuck dealing with the prim little Icelandic man all by myself. I say "man," though he is probably close to my age. But he exudes grownupness in a way I never will. I bet he was born in a suit.

He asked me how I slept in that generic way that customer service people do. You know they don't really care about the answer. I sure as shit don't whenever I politely ask mom's patients about their day. So I was just, like, "Fine." He gave me a key card for my new room—304. Top floor. The birch floor, yes! He also gave me a city bus pass and a stack of brochures to look over.

And then he took out a little notebook and pen and went, "What is the purpose of your trip?"

And I was, like, "Sorry, dude, I didn't know I had to

explain myself to a bellhop." Okay, no, I didn't say it like that. But I didn't really have an answer for him.

What is my purpose, Vivian?

He wrote something in Icelandic in his notebook, then went on to explain that he was my personal concierge and that it was his job to see to it I had a pleasant trip. He said he could do things like book sightseeing tours for me, or recommend restaurants, or whatever. I asked if he was doing this because I had to sleep on the roof, because I was fine with sleeping on the roof even if the temperature got down to sixteen FAHRENHEIT, and I didn't need any special treatment. And he said his services came with the hotel stay.

Oh, so that's why Mamochka picked this particular hotel. She wanted to make sure I was "having fun." She thought I needed a babysitter. Then it dawned on me.

"You talked to my mother, didn't you? Did she call here?"

"I don't think so. No." And oh my God, I need to take poker-face lessons from this guy.

"Talks like zhis," I said, putting on the Russian accent. "Probably called me her 'little baby boy.' Any of this ringing a bell?"

"No bells," he said. I thought for a moment his facade was going to crack, but he straightened up even more and repeated himself. "My services are included in your stay."

"All right, man. I'll look these over," I said, waving the stack of brochures, "and let you know if I feel the urge to swim with the orcas or go snorkeling with puffins or whatever."

"Thank you." He got up and pushed in his chair, giving me a little bow. And then — I shit you not — he stole a piece of toast right off my plate and ate it on his way out the door.

Miles Away to Vivian Girl

June 3 2:15 PM

I've just spent twenty minutes trying to figure out how to flush an Icelandic toilet. Ugh! I swear, I was this close to phoning the front desk and asking Man-Bun how to dispose of my piss. He probably gets asked that a lot. I can imagine him all straight-faced, like, *Place your palm against the large white button and push.* There are no handles or knob or anything — that's what I kept looking for. Seriously, it turned out to be a HUGE button. So huge that I overlooked it completely. I thought that thing was like a tissue dispenser or something. Push — flush — crisis averted. Of course I didn't have this problem last night because the toilets in the spa were auto-flush.

I'm in my room now. I went back to the roof after breakfast and grabbed my stuff. It had started to rain again, so I was kind of glad to settle into someplace with an actual ceiling. And this room is super pretty. You'd love it. There's this big mural on the wall behind my bed, a birch tree forest with beams of sunlight shining down.

I figured since I'm going to be here awhile, I might as well unpack. Put away my toiletries in the bathroom, clothes in the dresser. That's when I stopped to piss and got stumped by the toilet. Hopefully that's my last hurdle of the day.

Miles Away to Vivian Girl

June 3 2:47 PM

Nooooo. No. No. No. No. No. Vivian. You won't believe what just happened to me. I went to log on to Netflix, and the screen said *We're sorry, Netflix is not available in your country.* Is this hell?! Am I in hell?!

Miles Away to Vivian Girl

June 3 3:57 PM

I was just at the hotel's art gallery. Nothing too interesting. It's a small room, and a lot of the work in there was chess-themed because apparently Bobby Fischer won that really big tournament here. But, anyway, off the side of the gallery, you can head out into this enclosed garden, and that was the part that was pretty cool. There are these small, gnarly trees, and some street artists had wrapped their trunks in bright Icelandic wool. So everything looks kind of like a weird-ass cross between a Dr. Seuss book and something Tim Burton-y.

In the center, there's a koi pond with a little bridge that goes across. And on the bridge there are a zillion multicolored padlocks. It's a lover's bridge, like that famous one in Paris, where couples are supposed to put the lock on together and throw the key into the water below. At the gift shop in the hotel lobby I bought a purple lock and key.

Lock on the bridge. *Snap.*

Key in the water. *Plop.*

Oh, and what's that other noise? Just my heart cracking in half.

Hey, do you remember the first time we said I love you? Because I sure as hell don't. Seems like that's probably a big moment for most couples. I guess that's one of the downfalls of becoming romantically involved with a person who's practically been a family member for so long. The I-Love-You-Like-a-Siblings bleed into I-Love-You-You're-My-Soulmate, and you almost feel cheated a little bit.

Nah, I don't really mean that. I don't feel cheated. We had a pretty awesome relationship. And, yeah, you weren't there today to put that lock on the bridge, but hey, there's still that overpass where you spray-painted our names.

That's another day I think about a lot. I was just having one of those lazy-in-bed-in-my-underwear kind of Saturdays, and you showed up and made me get dressed so we could go for a walk. Walking down the street, I felt like I always did whenever I was beside you: a little taller and more sure of myself. You had a magic I hadn't seen in anyone else before or since, and it rubbed off on everything you touched. Could that be what happened? You gave and gave and gave to everyone else until there wasn't any more of that sparkle left for you.

It was springtime, cold and cloudy that day because Missouri only has two seasons: arctic and armpit. We hadn't hit the sweaty balls season yet. Anyway, you dragged me up over the viaduct into the park. There was a birthday party going on, little kids running around in pointy paper hats.

I played on the swings for the first time in a while and discovered that after all those years away from the playground, when you jump out of a swing, that long second of weightlessness still exists.

You just hit a liiiittle harder coming down now.

"I wanna show you something," you said, while I tried to dust the grass stains off my knees. You hadn't swung with me because you didn't want to rough up your dress. You were particular about your clothes, carefully curating each item from thrift shops and vintage sellers online. I never saw you buy anything new or expensive, but you treated every dress like it was spun from gold. I think that day you were wearing that short dress with the lacy overlay we'd dyed yellow in the kitchen sink one day with turmeric and Rit. Black fishnets and ballet flats.

We walked to the edge of the park with that big ditch, and I said, "Let me show you something first." And I pointed to that little green house on the other side with the dormers and told you it was once my great-great-grandma's house.

"I know," you said. "The Irish lady. And her husband was full-blooded Cherokee. She'd call him 'that old Indian' whenever she got mad."

"Yeah. How'd you know that?"

"Your mom told me. She said it's why she calls Mamochka 'that old Russian' sometimes." You were running your palms over the tops of the high grass that grew along the ditch. "The casual racism in your family is so cute."

"Hey, my family's history of ethnically intermixed romance made the Missouri mutt standing before you today. I'm Russian and Irish and Cherokee and Dutch and all kinds of other shit."

"I know. That's why it's so great," you said, glancing back toward the little green house across the way. "I think about them a lot. I bet it wasn't easy for them, you know? Her dad probably wanted her to marry the banker's son or something, and she was, like, *No way, I want that brown guy with the killer cheekbones.* I mean, I bet people threw shit at them out their buggy windows on Saturday night, and they still just did their thang."

I cringed a little, remembering that time some asshole in a Jeep decided we needed the rest of his milkshake.

Then I grabbed you and put my head on your shoulder, and we stood like that for a little while until I remembered you'd said you wanted to show me something.

"You're blind," you said. "I can't believe you haven't noticed it yet."

So I looked around and that's when I saw MILES + VIVIAN etched on the side of the overpass beneath the bridge.

"Oh my God. We've got to get out of here," I said, turning tail. "Wha—why would you do that? We're gonna get arrested. I'm pretty damn sure that you and I are the only 'Miles plus Vivian' in town."

"Oh, relax!" you said, tugging on my arm. "Nobody's getting arrested."

"How do you know? Once somebody sees that, the cops'll be knocking on our door."

And you said, "Miles, it's been there for, like, two years."

"Two years?" We'd only had our first kiss, like, six months before that.

"Oh yeah," you said, hands on your hips. "Been crushin' on you for a while now. When I was little, I used to go to the corner store and sneak a peek at *Seventeen* magazine the same way the other boys might try to see some tits in *Playboy*. Anyway, there was this article about positive affirmations. I didn't get to read the whole thing, because someone came around the corner and I threw it back on the shelf before they saw me. But I remember it said if you want something, you gotta write it down. I used to steal Nikki's diaries—not to read them, but to have a place where I could write *I want to be a girl, I want to be me,* over and over again under lock and key. Anyway, I still do that shit. If I want something, I write it down."

So I looked back up at your giant affirmation and grinned. I held you, and I told you I loved you. And you said it back. We'd said it to each other before, but now that I'm really thinking about it, this might have been the first time it meant something else.

I've pored over your art journals this past year and a half. I know it wouldn't bother you that I've read them. I think you were happy to be able to keep them out in the open, unlocked. Some of them are cheerful, and some of them are silly. And there are a few where you were obviously feeling sad, but nothing that seemed to raise any alarms.

I've looked everywhere, but you didn't leave a note when you tried to kill yourself. I don't know why.

I wish I did.

Miles Away to Vivian Girl

June 4 5:30 PM

Iceland. Day Three. Still jet-lagged as hell. I didn't get to sleep until around six a.m., but the phone woke me up at noon.

Peppy male voice on the other end says, "Good afternoon! This is your personal concierge. I was wondering if I could do anything for you today?"

Half asleep, I go, "I don't know. Can I have a different teapot? Mine's kind of fu   not working right." I tried using it last night to make some ramen I bought at the gas station, but it wouldn't work, so I had a bag of Skittles for dinner.

"Your electric kettle?" There is something magical about the way Icelandic people speak. It's soft and sharp all at the same time. Smooth vowels, long rolling r's and prickly k's: "electrrrreK Kayh-tul."

"Yeah. It's, like, rusted or something."

"Sorry to hear that. A new kettle it is! Anything else? Some tea?"

"Nah. I was just going to make some noodles."

"Noodles? Yes, yes. I'll bring you a bowl."

"Cool. Thanks . . . uh, *takk*." Literally the only Icelandic word I know.

And then, like, two minutes later, Man-Bun was at my door with an electric kettle under his arm and a full set of kitchenware on a tray. So nice. I feel bad about secretly mocking his hair all the time. I let him in because he wanted to take the old kettle and make sure the other one, which he'd borrowed from an empty room down the hall, was working. While we were literally waiting for water to boil, I showed him the ramen I bought at the gas station yesterday.

"It's funny. I heard you all speak English, and you do," I said.

"Yes." He said it almost like a question, or maybe as though he was expecting the punch line to a bad joke. I can't say I like this guy, but it is sort of amusing the way he and I have no clue what to make of each other.

"But some of the food packaging is in Icelandic. I can't tell if this is vegetarian or not. Do you mind?" It had an illustration of vegetables on the package, as opposed to the other varieties the store carried that displayed a chicken drumstick and a smiling pig.

"You don't eat any meat?" He looked the packaging over. "There's a bit of egg in it."

"Egg is fine," I said.

"No meat." He handed the package back just as the kettle whistled.

"It's working!" I said, excited about my ramen. Ah, a home-cooked meal . . .

"You can't just eat noodles all month," he said. "You'll get scurvy."

"Scurvy?" I dumped the ramen into the water, pulled up the timer on my phone, and set it for three minutes. "The pirate disease?"

"Yes. A vitamin C deficiency." He headed for the door and gave me a little wave. "Be sure to eat some citrus fruits."

"All right. I will." I laughed. "Thanks, man. I'm sorry. I didn't catch your name yet. I've been so jet-lagged."

He pointed to his little bronze name tag. ÓSKAR.

"Thanks, Óskar." I said it like Oscar. American-style.

He shook his head. "No. Oh-skargh." I swear— just like that. No wonder these Scandinavian languages sound so absurd to American ears. How the hell does Óskar have a g and an h in it?

So, I tried. "Thanks, Oskjdlmfjaiejtjoughai."

And he, like, cuffed me on the shoulder with the broken teapot. "You will get the hang of it."

I ate my noodles and went back to sleep. When I woke up later, there was a mesh bag of oranges hanging on my doorknob.

Miles Away to Vivian Girl
June 4 11:33 PM

It's hard to really gauge how much I think about you. On the one hand, constantly. It's sort of like that feeling when you know you've forgotten something important. That foreboding feeling that just hangs with you. Of course I haven't forgotten anything about you. I still remember your voice and your laugh and the way you smell. But it's a feeling that, in remembering, I'll lose everything.

So, on the other hand, it's best not to think about you. Not to let that black cloud sink any lower. Because if I do let those thoughts in, I drown.

You can imagine what kind of day it's been.

It's hard being here without you. But I think I understand part of the reason my moms sent me away. It's easier to reboot in a strange place.

And that makes me think of you, which makes the idea starting over as Miles 2.0 a bit harder. Of meeting you for the first time. In person, I mean. We'd been friends online for a while, always staying up way too late messaging each other and swapping project ideas for *Mixtape*. You were constantly getting me in trouble, Vivian, by making me laugh so hard Mamochka would wake up and make me turn my phone off.

And then there was that one night you called. We texted sometimes, but you never called me, so I was a little freaked out.

Plus, it was, like, three a.m.

"I did something so stupid," you said as soon as I picked up. Your voice was soft and trembling, and you had a slight

Southern accent, which never made sense because I don't have an accent and I live farther south. "I ran away from home."

I buried my nose in my pillow for a second, then turned my face back toward the phone. "Where are you?"

"How far away is Poplar Bluff?"

"From where?"

"From you."

"Are you in Poplar Bluff?"

"Everything looked a lot closer on the map, and I thought I'd just figure it out when I got here, but it's really creepy and dark, and I don't think I can walk that far."

"Are you seriously in Poplar Bluff?"

"Yes. I took an Amtrak. I'm an idiot. I just really want to meet you and go to your camp and hug your stupid awesome parents. Do you know how lucky you are? Your life is like a dream to me."

So, then I had to go wake my parents up and explain to them that an online stranger was waiting for me at the train station half an hour away. But I am lucky. And I do have stupid awesome parents, the kind of parents who understand that life is sometimes so shitty that you have to take a train to nowhere in the middle of the night and hope a friend you've never met will rescue you.

Mom went to get you. In the meantime, she called the police to sit with you until she arrived. And she called your parents to let them know where you were, that you were okay.

I wanted to go with her when she picked you up, but Mom told me to go back to bed since it was a school night. Of course I couldn't sleep. Mamochka and I waited up in the living room, staring at late-night infomercials with bleary eyes.

When I heard Mom's car pull up, I ran out into the yard and met you as you were coming up the driveway.

I will admit now that I was momentarily confused. I thought there'd been a mix-up, some misunderstanding.

Your voice came out high-pitched and rapid. "Don't look much like my avatar, do I? I wanted to tell you sooner. Please don't be mad. I'm sorry."

It's true, you didn't look how I expected at all. Even though, growing up with my parents, I'd met trans people before, it still took me a couple seconds to untangle my thoughts. I'm sorry about that moment, by the way. That pause, like I'm sure everyone else in the world had always done, when my brain insisted on categorizing you on appearance alone: a fellow fat guy, sweating in a black hoodie and jeans. Then everything clicked: the reason for the cartoon profile picture, your fascination with my parents and Camp, and the fact that you'd chosen my gender identities comic for your mag.

Okay, my brain said. *Trans. Got it.*

I threw my arms around you and said I didn't care. "It's so cool to finally meet you, Vivian."

Then you were crying. Mom's headlights were shining on your face, and I could see then that you were definitely not just another guy like me. You had the prettiest face. No makeup at all, and your hair was in those little braids so that your parents wouldn't give you shit about growing it out.

You wiped your eyes and said, "No one's ever called me that name before. I mean, not in person. Not out loud."

I don't think you slept at all that night. You must have spent the whole time untangling your cornrows. And when you showed up at breakfast the next morning in your 1950s secretary dress with your messy, fluffy hair, you kind of blew my mind. I couldn't imagine someone could change so much overnight.

Things went downhill after that. My parents took you back home and tried to talk to your family. We were hoping your parents would let you come back with us for Camp, but they just grounded you. They took away your internet privileges, and I didn't hear from you again for months and months.

I'll never forget that first morning, though. You were glowing, and you were really happy to be somewhere new. In our kitchen, in that dress, you finally were yourself, but in my eyes you became someone new.

I wish I knew how to do that.

Tomorrow. Maybe tomorrow I'll wake up fully recharged and ready to explore.

Miles Away to Vivian Girl

June 5 9:18 AM

Okay. So, I could really use your help right now. The real

reason I haven't ventured any farther than the corner store in the three days since I've been here is that . . . I don't really understand city buses. I mean, we don't have public transportation at home, you know? I caught Brian online a few minutes ago and asked him how buses work. He was like, "With an engine, Miles. Duh." And then he also went on to say that Icelandic buses are probably powered by mystical elfin technology. And, of course, I was like, "That's not what I mean, you ass-wipe." I guess I don't understand bus routes. Like, how do I know where the bus will take me? God, I'm stupid, right?

You're from St. Louis. I remember you talking about riding buses around the city. I bet you could easily figure out how to get from point A to point B around here, but I've got no clue. It's entirely possible I'll never see more of Reykjavik than the inside of this hotel if I don't figure this shit out.

Miles Away to Vivian Girl

June 5 4:14 PM

I had a great morning, Vivian. Really cool. I'm grinning about this morning, happy for the first time in such a long while.

After I messaged you earlier, I got dressed, crammed my bus pass and map into my pocket, and decided that I was going to put my ass on a bus that looked like it was going toward town and see what the hell would happen.

I glanced at the front desk as I was leaving, but Óskar

wasn't there. I'm not sure if it was a good or bad thing that my Mamochka-appointed babysitter wasn't around to see me finally getting the heck out of Dodge.

So, I sat in the little glass bus stop thingy and waited, my heart going nine thousand BPM. A bus showed up. I flashed my pass at the driver, then climbed aboard. My knees felt all wobbly, so I was super glad there were free seats and I didn't have to stand there clinging to a pole like a stripper with stage fright.

There was this woman who boarded the bus right after me. I looked at her once or twice out of the corner of my eye and thought . . . *Do I know her?* She looked a hell of a lot like this girl who used to babysit me . . . no way. But I kept looking at her and she kept looking at me, and finally she goes, "Well, say something! One of us has to!"

I got even more flustered then. "Uh, you are Shannon . . . right?"

"Yes! Come over here, Miles." She patted the empty seat next to her.

How totally weird, right? I have vague memories of her teaching me how to make grilled cheese and us dancing around the house to Mamochka's Cyndi Lauper records. Man, that seems like such a long time ago.

I sat next to Shannon, and she gave me this huge hug, but I made it sort of awkward because I couldn't figure out which way to turn my face and almost smashed my forehead into her nose.

"This is so bizarre. Same hotel and everything? How long have you been here? It's a wonder we haven't run into each other before."

"I know. Strange," I said, brushing off her question because I didn't want to tell her how freaked out I'd been about leaving my room.

"What are you doing here, Miles?" She laughed and slapped my arm, but then her face fell. "Oh, never mind. I've been following the story on the news. I just had this horrible breakup—not that it's anything like what you're going through . . . I am so sorry. How are you holding up?"

I remember my hands were in my lap and my fists were clenched so tight. I forced myself to relax a little, stretching out my fingers. The last thing I needed was another damn panic attack. "I've been better."

"Me, too," she said.

She looked the same as she used to. She's got long curly hair down to her ass and a killer smile. Dresses all bohemian with long skirts and flowery patterns. I definitely had a crush on her back in the day. And it was definitely coming back to me. Such a strange feeling, like my insides had gotten a little lighter, but outwardly I was gawky and blushing. I guess I haven't grown up much at all.

She didn't seem to notice that I'd reverted to my eleven-year-old self, a hot mess of hormones and bad hair. She patted my shoulder, and the rest of me went up in flames. She said, "I'm getting better every day, though. And you will, too."

We talked a little bit more. Shannon said she was leaving to go back home tomorrow, then asked if I was doing anything today. When I shrugged, she invited me along to go souvenir shopping downtown. I said I would, happy I didn't have to blindly find my way into the city. Though, once we got off the bus, I admitted to her that I had no clue how to get around. She told me that buses run on a loop. You just have to get on the right one headed the right direction, then get off at the stop closest to your destination. Makes sense.

"I'm so dumb. Oh God! Am I a redneck?" I tugged at the collar of my T-shirt.

She laughed that stupid sexy laugh. "I like your shirt, by the way. It's deflecting."

"Precisely my point," I said. You haven't seen this shirt, V. I got it a few months ago. It's light gray with dark blue cuffs around the collar and sleeves, and the print is dark blue, too. It says YOU ARE A TOURIST, like that Death Cab for Cutie song.

So, we ended up walking around Laugavegur, the main shopping district. The streets downtown are brick, and I kept stumbling over myself on the uneven path. It's pretty there, urban and hip. Lots of street art and little boutiques.

We went in a million little trinket shops, and I helped her pick out souvenirs for her friends back home. We laughed at the stupid T-shirts and postcards that covered topics like Icelandic volcano name pronunciations and the ever-changing weather.

"If you don't like the weather in Iceland, just wait a few minutes. We say that in Missouri, too," Shannon told a shopkeeper.

Mostly we just talked. And not about you. It seems like every conversation in my life over the past year and a half has circled around to you, but these didn't. I told her a bunch of stupid jokes, and she laughed at them. I stood too close to her. And she let me.

I grinned. I grinned so much my face hurts.

Hello, world. Do you remember this guy? This version of Miles, the bizarre and the bold? He's back and looking to score.

And he might, actually . . . with his super-hot former babysitter. (Okay, she's eight years older than me. But twenty-six isn't that old, is it? She sure as shit doesn't look twenty-six.) She asked me out tonight, though. Something about a northern lights tour by boat. I don't know. I wasn't really listening. I was just watching her lips move.

chapter six

Miles Away to Vivian Girl

June 6 2:53 AM

Oh, V. My Vivian Girl. I am back from my night out, and your boots are kicked off in the corner of my room, and I am a little drunk. From stolen boozy apple cider on a boat in the middle of the Atlantic. And after everything that's happened tonight, I am thinking about your mouth . . . you. Your lips against mine and the way you used to kiss my ears and run your tongue around the edge of my gauges and that little crunchy sound it made when you bit down on the shell of my ear. I get shivers thinking about that, even now. I don't know how to stop being so in love with you.

And because I am drunk on stolen cider and feeling sloppy and romantic, I'll tell you everything about tonight, all right?

I didn't sleep with her.

Fuck I wanted to.

So, after we did all her shopping, we went back to the hotel and Shannon wanted to stop at the desk and get me a ticket for the northern lights thing. There were a few concierges at the front desk, and Óskar was busy, but she wanted to wait for him because she thinks they probably work off commission and she likes Óskar the best. She said he's a perfect man because he makes sure she has a bottle of wine delivered to her room at the end of every night. I told her Óskar was a toast thief; therefore, not to be trusted.

Anyway, after he was done getting an elderly Asian couple set up with a rental car, Shannon had Óskar print us off some vouchers. I remember he had a black Sharpie pen tucked behind his ear, and there was a collapsed Jenga tower scattered across his desk. When he handed me my voucher, he said, "You have finally decided to leave the hotel?" and then he blinked at me in that way cats do—wide-eyed and completely uninterested in your life. He also seemed rather unimpressed by the fact that two people from the same small town in Missouri had randomly met in a hotel in another corner of the planet. What. A. Weirdo.

After that, me and Shannon parted ways for a while. She said she needed to go cram all her souvenirs into her suitcases. I read in my room. Ate some oranges. Took a shower. Fixed my hair. Crawled on the ceiling in anticipation, you know . . .

We met in the lobby at eleven thirty. A van picked us up and took us to the harbor. Everything was this dark blue color, the sky, the water. It looked like a van Gogh painting, the way the city lights reflected out in long lines across the waves.

I wanted to draw it. No, paint it. I wanted to smear

blue-black mess across a canvas and make little yellow and white squiggles for all the light. I needed you there with me right then, because I didn't think anyone else would understand that some things cannot be replicated with words or photos even. Sometimes light and memories work that way. Like you can only understand them if they leave stains on your hands.

I think encaustic painting might be good for the harbor landscape I saw tonight. Sometimes I watch YouTube tutorials on painting and shit. It's really interesting and comforting. Sometimes it puts me right to sleep. But, anyway, encaustics. It's painting with melted beeswax and dye. I think I want to try that sometime. Sometime when I figure out how the hell I can get back to making art again.

We were some of the first people on the boat, this big whaleboat-looking rig. (I wish I'd paid attention to the name. Boat names are always cool.) Apparently Shannon's super into this aurora-hunting thing: "This is my third time on this tour. They refund your ticket if you don't see the lights, and no luck so far, so I keep coming back. Tonight's my last chance."

She asked me if I'd ever seen the northern lights, and I said only technically. Mom and Mamochka told me we all saw them on a trip to Montana one time, but I was just a little kid. The only thing I remember about that trip was that I got really carsick and threw up in a Big Gulp cup. Great job prioritizing the memories, brain.

I followed her down a set of stairs to one of the viewing cabins, where there are big picture windows and dining tables.

There were also racks and racks of those big *Deadliest Catch*–looking jumpsuits for anybody who wanted to keep warm while hanging out on the open-air deck up top. Shannon pulled one on over her swishy dress, but she looked so unsexy in that getup that she was unable to convince me to do the same. "You'll freeeeze!"

I had a hoodie, so I figured I'd be fine. Wrong. I was miserably cold all night.

We went up a level to another viewing room where there were all kinds of drinks and snacks on a table and in coolers. Shannon grabbed a couple of candy bars and a few cans of hard apple cider and we climbed our way to the open deck at the very top. Closer to the stars.

"Should we, uh, pay for that loot?" I said when Shannon handed me a can.

"No one cares," she said.

"Sure, no one cares. If you're a beautiful woman. But I'm a pudgy postadolescent in need of a haircut."

"Miles, I don't know if you've noticed, but you're not pudgy anymore. You do need a haircut, though." She paused and looked me over. "How much weight have you lost?"

"Uh, I'm not sure. A lot." I smoothed my hand over where my gut used to be. Just like you haven't seen my Tourist T-shirt, you haven't seen the slowly shrinking guy inside of it.

"So far my breakup has made me gain ten pounds."

"You'd think I'd like how my body looks now, but I kinda miss the old me. At least I was happy then." I leaned against the railing as the deck filled with passengers and the boat shoved off. I kept staring down at the waves, imagining myself slipping between the bars and into that cold, black water.

Someone would rescue me if I fell in, wouldn't they? They'd give me a blanket and cocoa and I'd be just fine, right?

I drank my stolen booze and felt a little guilty thrill. I held on to that railing tight.

"So, tell me about this website," Shannon said.

"I don't know. It was just this idea that Vivian had. It used to be a blog, but she expanded it into an online magazine. She wanted to create a space where all these artsy misfit kids could connect online. It's called *Mixtape*, 'cause she was huge on nineties pop culture, like riot grrrl music and stuff. Anyway, every month, she'd pick a theme—like water or dignity or something—and people would create a piece of art based on the theme. Like a drawing or poetry or whatever. And there was lots of collaboration all around. It got kinda super popular for a minute there, and I helped her run everything. We even got a book deal."

"Really? You got a book published?"

"Kinda. I drew some coloring pages and helped with the art design and stuff. I don't know. It was mostly Vivian's thing."

"And what's your thing?" she asked. The wind whipped her hair against my cheek.

"My thing," I said, "was making Vivian happy. But I guess I wasn't too good at that."

I thought maybe Shannon would drop the subject the way Brian does when I tend to get all Eeyore about things. But she didn't. She looked at me and said, "That's not an answer. Or not a good one."

I squinted and said, "What? How?"

"I get the feeling, Miles," she said, tugging on my sleeve so I'd turn and look at her, "I get the feeling that nobody is asking you to be a grownup about this. Your mom's a child psychologist, so she's probably treating you like one of her patients. And your other mom—I know because I've seen her do it—still calls you her baby boy, yeah?"

"Yeah."

"So, don't let them give you a pacifier."

Because I was starting to get a little buzzed, I laughed.

And Shannon whacked me on the chest. "I mean it. Don't let anyone's expectations define what happiness means for you. Especially not your parents. And especially not a coma patient!"

And that hit me so hard. In feels I didn't even know I had anymore. I pulled my hoodie a little tighter. But that didn't stop the wind from dragging tears out of my eyes and cooling them on my cheeks.

"You cannot make her happy anymore. You virtually cannot."

"Okay. I get it," I said, dragging my cuff across my face. "No more, okay? Not tonight."

She nodded and crushed her cider can under her heel, then stuffed it into the pocket of her jumpsuit because there were no trashcans in sight.

There was a tour guide, a burly ginger dude with a microphone who was full of folktales and history. He told stories all night and read this poem about the northern lights. I can't remember a word of it, but it was beautiful.

And I had a few more apple-y beverages. After we finished off the first few, I went below deck and bought us some more. I don't even think I'm old enough, but no one asked for an ID. I also paid for the other cans we'd sort of stolen. I know. Lame. But you can't change Rome in a night, or what the fuck ever that saying is. At least I had some drinks. And good thing they tasted more like apples than beer, because . . . well, you know why. I can't stand the smell of booze since you.

After the aurora poem, Shannon leaned on my shoulder. I told her thanks for getting me out of the hotel. It wasn't bad, really, doing this touristy thing.

Summer is a shitty time for catching the aurora, what with only, like, two hours of darkness each night. But, somehow, an hour or so after we'd been out there, the guide told us to look over to the west. There it was, just these faint green swirls. Fingers, he called them. Everyone scrambled for their big clunky cameras, even Shannon.

"Don't be stupid," I slurred. "Just look at it." It was so faint, and the sun was about to crest. I knew it was pointless to try to capture it on camera. I could have easily got up on my soapbox about MEMORIES OVER MEGAPIXELS and how everyone thinks their experiences are invalid unless they post them in full color on Facebook, but I didn't. I didn't say anything else. But she knew. And that's probably why, when the lights finally faded and everyone put their cameras down, my hot former babysitter kissed me.

We didn't talk about it. The boat turned around, and we went to the lower decks to warm up. There were a couple of teenage girls down there with guitars singing gorgeous Icelandic folk songs. I wish I could describe this to you better, but I really can't. Except to say that it was pretty and . . . ethereal, maybe? And that I felt really all right.

It was two a.m. when we got back to shore. The sun came up and there were cars and people everywhere in downtown Reykjavik. I guess if we were cooler, Shannon and I could have stayed out and done the *rúntur,* that late-night Icelandic barhopping I'd heard about. But she had an early flight, so we just went back to the hotel.

In the elevator, I said to her that I'd be stupid not to at least ask if she wanted to come to my room. She laughed and said, "I really do have an early flight."

"Aw, come on. I just need, like, ten minutes tops."

"But I'm a grown-ass woman. I need a little longer than that."

"Wait, are we talking about sleep or sex? I'm drunk."

"Sex. But it's the same for sleep, too. I don't not want to have sex with you, Miles. Just . . . not tonight?" The elevator stopped at her floor.

"I totally respect that garbled nonsense could I please kiss you some more?" I grabbed her hand. The doors closed, and we went up, smashing our drunken faces into each other.

I may have gotten to second base.

We kept kissing, but when the elevator stopped at my floor, she broke away and pushed her button again. We rode back down, and she moaned like a banshee when I nibbled on her bottom lip. And then she got out when the elevator stopped.

"I admire your self-control," I said. "But I weep for those who value sleep more than sex."

"You'll understand when you're older," she said. "Hey, look me up when you get back home. Maybe we'll continue this on American soil."

"You don't mean that," I said. "Good night."

"Night." She grinned, and I grinned.

Maybe she meant it. Maybe she didn't.

I dunno.

Maybe I will call her when I get back home.

chapter seven

Miles Away to Vivian Girl

June 6 11:14 AM

The sunlight gets into everything here. It just barges through the curtains whenever it pleases. My body still doesn't understand what time it is. So, I think the healing properties of Icelandic sunshine might be having the opposite effect on me.

I am on that slippery edge again, Vivian. Last night I felt amazing, and today I'm wallowing. I feel like shit. I'm not hung-over or anything. I'm just a shitty person.

What was I thinking? No, I wasn't thinking. And that's the problem.

Or it's the solution.

All I know is that I want to have more nights like last night and fewer mornings like this one. The trick is to keep moving, I think, and to focus on me instead of you. Shannon was probably right about happiness, that no one else can validate it for me. Mamochka thinks the same thing, too. The other day she told me if I was feeling selfish, I was probably doing things right. "Because you need to take care of yourself right now, little baby boy."

Funny how she can tell me to take care of myself and call me baby in the same sentence.

There is something that happened last night that I don't know quite how to explain to you, or even if I should. It wasn't the drinking or the aurora, or the kissing even. It was much later, when I was back in my room. Starting to sober up and feeling so stupid and sad. I sat up on the edge of my bed, and there were your boots. They were standing up, just as I'd pulled them off. So empty without you. I kept staring at them, like if I looked hard enough, all this shit would suddenly make sense. And, then, after all my bitching about megapixels and shit, what did I do? I grabbed my phone and took a picture.

And the thing is, taking that photo felt good. As good as a kiss.

You know, I thought I needed somewhere safe and quiet to curl up and lick my wounds, but maybe I've done that enough already? I want more of those stupid/giddy/lusty feelings, and I'm pretty sure I'm not going to get them alone in my hotel room. So I'm going out.

To do my laundry.

Ha ha, okay, so I'm making that sound lamer than it is. There's this place downtown called the Laundromat Cafe, where I can, in fact, do my laundry, but also chill out and people watch in the café part. There's some veggie food on the menu, and the place is stocked with tons of books. I'm not taking my iPad, and my phone's been on airplane mode this whole trip. (Emergencies only! Since we don't have an international plan.) Should keep me from staring at Tumblr all day and messaging the void. Later, V.

Miles Away to Vivian Girl
June 8 9:14 AM

Hahahahahahah. Ha. I don't know whether to laugh or cry about my brilliant idea to Venture Bravely Forth into the World. You may have noticed (pfff) I haven't messaged in a while. That's because I haven't actually been in Reykjavik since I last messaged you. Yeah, because I decided it was totally a good idea to hitch a ride HALFWAY ACROSS ICELAND with a bunch of random strangers. That happened. God.

So, starting from the beginning now. Another installment in the New Icelandic Saga of Miles.

The Laundromat Cafe is really damn cool, actually. You go downstairs, toss your stuff in the wash (a girl at the hotel desk set me up with some Icelandic coinage — krónur have fish on them instead of dead politicians) and then head back up to the café. I ordered this eggplant sandwich thingy. So good. I also had a chai tea and tried to flirt with my waitress. I might as well have been chatting with a cactus.

So, I gave up and started browsing the café's color-coded bookshelves. And then, there it was, suddenly and unexpectedly. A slim magenta spine with LOFTIS down the side. The first of two times this weekend I was surprised to see your name.

Of course. Of fucking course this hipster café in Reykjavik, Iceland, has a copy of *Mixtape*'s anthology. I flicked through the pages until I found the section in the back that I'd contributed: the junkyard coloring book pages. It looked pretty much like you'd expect a coloring book to look after being left in a public place. There were wide green scribbles across full spreads where clumsy-fingered toddlers had been given full artistic range. Also, ink pen doodles of hairy-balled cocks here and there. Thankfully some of the pages had been colored properly by someone who knew their way around art supplies.

After my weird fantasies in the showers the other night, I did sort of get the illusion of being caught in public with my dick in my hand when I looked up from the book I'd helped create and saw someone staring at me. Someone kind of attractive.

You'd think that growing up in my house, I'd have a better understanding of human sexuality. At the very least, I ought to be able to figure out my own. I know I land somewhere on the demisexuality spectrum, because I don't always notice whether or not I'm physically attracted to someone until I really get to know them. My brain tends to make a few exceptions, though. Like, um, there was that one summer that I realized a few of Brian's teammates looked really good in their baseball uniforms. I had to stop going to the games because, goddamn. The last thing I needed was a crush on a bunch of straightboy jocks.

Anyway, the other exception to this rule (besides tight baseball pants) is that lately I've been finding myself drawn to gender nonconformity. I'm sure Mom could analyze that all day, and it probably does say something about my attachment to you. On the other hand, I'd like to say for the record that you always looked like a girl to me, even when you had to present as a boy. You didn't put off that tough, boy/girl aura I've been intrigued by lately. Not like the person staring at me in the Laundromat.

"Whatcha reading?" They were sitting in a squishy beanbag-type chair by the window. This thin, attractive person of ambiguous gender. Spiky teal-tipped hair. Vaguely Asian-looking, American-ish accent.

"Oh, this?" I said, like a dork. I plopped into the next bean chair over and showed them the cover of your book. "My girlfriend and I put this together."

Then I remembered that flirting usually doesn't involve mentioning to the new person that you have a girlfriend.

"I mean, I guess she's not my girlfriend anymore. It's . . ."

"Complicated?" they said.

I shrugged.

"Wait. Is that *Mixtape*?" They grabbed the book out of my hands. "I read that." A pause as they handed it back and something must have clicked in their head. "Oh my God, you're Vivian's boyfriend? Um, Milo?"

"Miles."

"Right! Miles! I love *Mixtape*. Good stuff." They nodded and sipped their coffee. In the window behind them, I could see a young couple arguing on the street. I got that pain in my gut. I know it's stupid, but I miss having someone to argue with. "It's gone now, right? Such a shame, really. What happened?"

"Legal bullshit, pretty much. Domain expired. Lots of red tape to get it back," I said, keeping it short and sweet. "So, um, loyal reader. You got a name? Pronoun?"

"I think I'm feeling like a she today." She stuck out a hand. "Frankie."

I put down my tea and shook her hand. Funny, isn't it? I just have queer in my bones. The LGBT community can and will find me, wherever I roam. Anyway, we got to talking, and Frankie said she'd taken a year off from uni to travel. I always hear about kids doing this, but I don't understand how in the hell they can afford it. Me staying overseas for a month seems absurd! A year? Wow.

"Saw you chatting up that waitress. You could not have picked a worse time to try to get with an Icelandic chick." Frankie tilted her head toward the bar where the snooty waitress was laughing with co-workers and making lattes.

I felt my cheeks turning red. I hadn't known I had an

audience for my pathetic attempt at flirting. "Oh yeah? Why is that?"

"She probably got laid just last night. And now she's pissy and hung over and ready for the workday to end so she can get out and do it all again tonight. If you want Icelandic pussy, you've got to catch 'em when they're smashed, man. Their legs are only open during 'normal business hours'—Friday and Saturday from two to five a.m."

I have to admit now that, yes, I did look at that horrible how-to-score-with-Icelandic-babes website that Brian told me about. And, yes, it does state that these beautiful Nordic women like it drunk and late, late at night.

"That's a pretty narrow time frame. Where will I find Icelandic pussy that will work around MY schedule?" (Lawd, if my mothers could hear me now!)

"Well, I suppose I could help you out. There are these French girls in my hostel—" Frankie followed me around the café as I slid your book back onto the shelf and went to check on my laundry.

"French girls? I like where this is going. Continue." I crammed my clothes in the dryer and loaded it up with coins.

In the corner, another tourist was unloading a sack of laundry into the wash. He tugged his pullover off, and his T-shirt rode up a little, revealing the smooth tanned skin of his lower back. I stared at him a little longer than I meant to.

Before too long, I'll be a full-on zombie. I'm starting to have serious cravings for human flesh.

"They are French feminist graffiti artists. Even better, right?" Frankie leaned against one of the machines, looking sort of like a greaser in a 1950s movie. I guess that makes me Olivia Newton-John? "They don't speak any English or whatever, and I'm French-Canadian, so I've been helping them out a little. Anyway, we're going to tramp around town later and tag some stuff, then maybe go swimming. You up for it?"

"Yeah, sure," I said to Frankie. I wasn't sure about the graffiti, though. There's a lot of really beautiful street art in Reykjavik, and I wasn't sure if random people could paint up random places, but this huge part of me was like, *God, Miles, can you please just shut off your brain for a while?* Why not flirt with French girls and make my mark on something? It sounded like fun, and that's what I was supposed to be having, right? You'd have gone in a heartbeat. And, unlike me, you would've been okay.

But we'll get to that.

Frankie gave me directions to a skate park and told me to meet up with her when my clothes were finished, then she wandered off down the street. Once we were alone, the eye candy in the rumpled T-shirt smiled at me, but I couldn't tell if it meant something or not. Then four or five of his buddies showed up and started their laundry. They were talking about football in some European accent, and I decided he was probably straight.

And I had a bunch of French women waiting for me, right?

I spent the rest of my laundry time looking for a French phrase book. No luck. Finally the dryer stopped and I tossed it all in my bag. I should point out that, other than my swim trunks and maybe a spare pair of socks, this was every bit of clothing I'd packed for the entire trip. I decided to head straight for the skate park, rather than dropping my stuff off at the hotel. I was nervous and eager, afraid that if I took too long, they wouldn't be at the park when I got there.

But they were! Frankie and these two long-legged beauties. They were punky—one of them had that haircut where the side of her head was buzzed, and the other girl had a wicked septum piercing—but they both had these gauzy, flowy dresses on. In other words, they looked like music festival girls. I bet you a thousand bucks at least one of them owns a fake Native American headdress. Anyway, there wasn't much chitchat since I don't know a word of French. One of them handed me a plastic bag she'd been swinging around, and Frankie asked if I would stash it in my backpack for them. Inside was a manila envelope and three cans of spray paint. I managed to cram it all in my backpack and then we started walking around, looking for little secluded alleyways and interesting nooks for the girls to tag.

Now, when I think of graffiti artists, I tend to think of giant artsy murals, detailed work. These girls just had a couple of stencils. But whatever makes you feel like a badass, right?

And I did kinda. Feel like a badass, I mean. It was sort of

fun, especially when one of them wanted to climb up on my shoulders so she could paint some out-of-reach place.

Frankie and the French girls took turns tagging all over the city. A couple of times, one of them would try to pass a can over to me, and I'd politely wave my hands.

"Pussy," one of them said to me in English, loud and clear.

But it wasn't that. I wasn't so scared of getting caught. I could handle that. It might even be an interesting story to tell when I get back home. No, something else was holding me back.

I wasn't sure I could do it without you. It's hard to find the will to make something new and beautiful when I feel like a withering houseplant on the inside. Art was something you and I did together, passion to pass the time.

I will, reluctantly, tell you about the street art the French girls made, because if you were here with me, that's what you'd want to know. And, yes, you would have loved it.

First, a vine stencil. Green paint. *Clink, clink, clink, hissssss.* A stem. Next, pink paint through a petal-y stencil, the rose. Oh, but the rose is not a rose. It only looks like a rose if you aren't looking close enough. Actually, it was a vulva. Then the black paint, a framing piece. French words that Frankie translated to me. It's a Simone de Beauvoir quote. "One is not born a woman; one becomes one."

Yes, see? Like I said, you would have loved it. And I hate that so fucking much right now.

And so I never did take my turn with the stencils and paint. Instead, I pulled your boots off and snapped a cell phone picture of them next to one of the French girls' fresh tags. Frankie asked me what that was all about, so I said, "It's for Vivian."

"For Vivian," she repeated, all gravely. I just figured she thought it was sad. How gullible could a guy get? Though it's not like situations or people come with warning labels. No neon signs. No flashing lights.

Once the girls had had their fill of vandalism, the stencils went back into their envelope, and our priorities turned to the second set of plans for the evening: where to swim? Frankie and I asked around on the street until a local offered up an interesting enough sounding place. We walked to the hostel where the girls had a rental car, and we all piled in. The damn pool was an hour-and-a-half drive from Reykjavik, then a twenty-minute hike. But I was kind of enjoying myself. The scenery was pretty, and so were the French girls. I never even learned their names.

We followed the trail through the hills. I ended up lugging not only my backpack full of clothes and their spray paints, but also a cooler of beer that the French girls had brought along. And I had to piggyback one of them across a stream because she didn't want to get her precious little shoes wet. But, yeah, I enjoyed it at the time.

I stopped once more to photograph your empty boots against the pointed green hills that surrounded the valley. I don't know yet what the end result of these photos will be. I only know that taking them is starting to feel right.

So, this place . . . I'll have to Google it because all I can remember is that it starts with an *S*. It's Iceland's oldest swimming pool, or something. It's just this little secluded place. Nobody even maintains the pool anymore, so it's super murky and all natural. There's a building there—changing rooms, but they were disgusting. There's like an inch and a half of mud and moldy beer covering the floor of the place. I took off your boots and tied them together by the laces and hung them up on this hook outside the door. None of us actually changed in the changing rooms.

The French girls squealed and stripped and frolicked, as we all know French girls are wont to do. Frankie and I watched them splash in the pool as our jaws slowly unhinged. Slow-motion perfection. I started to feel like I'd snuck onto the set of a movie about the life of someone much cooler. One of the French girls had a rainbow peacock feather tattoo down her spine. God, I wanted to taste it.

Beside me, Frankie undressed too. AFAB, in case you were wondering. Zero shame about her body, though. Yeah, you heard me, Vivian. A non-gender-conforming stranger got completely, shamelessly nude in front of me, and the world did not end. And then I took my clothes off and dove into the water, trying to be as nonchalant and graceful as the three of them had managed.

Fast-forward a few beers. Frankie and the brunette were

putting their tongues down each other's throats. I was cozying up to the peacock girl, but I couldn't exactly bowl her over with my unique brand of wit. And, also, she was a lesbian. I asked Frankie to ask her, and she confirmed.

Well, damn. Who invited the straight(ish) guy?

More beer. Frankie had her head between the legs of the brunette, who was perched up on the ledge of the pool. I've never actually watched other people have sex, like, in person, before. I was mesmerized. The brunette squirmed, mouth open and head tilted back. She arched her back. Droplets of water trailed down the tendrils of wet hair that swirled around her breasts. I've never seen something so perfect in my life.

The peacock girl was watching, too. I tapped her shoulder, tilted my head toward Frankie and the brunette, then looked back at her. To my shock and delight, she shrugged and pulled herself up onto the ledge, spreading her legs for me. And I was happy to oblige.

(Sorry. Fuck. I just wish I could tell you these things for real. So you could scream or forgive. I don't know how I'm supposed to feel anymore. Is this cheating? I need you to tell me.)

But, the bad news is that I really have no clue how to go down on a girl. I mean, I guess this is a skill that I haven't had much of a chance to hone. So after just a few minutes, the peacock girl put her hand under my chin and lifted my face. She shook her head and sank back into the water.

Strike two, Miles.

I was thinking about that episode of *Seinfeld* where Elaine converts a gay guy, at least temporarily, but then finds out later that she's not as skilled as someone who has 24/7 "access to the equipment." I was bummed, but not being a lesbian turned out to be one of the lesser problems of my night.

I'm tired of typing for now. Ready to bury my head in the sand and nap for a while. Later I'll finish telling you this story. You know, the one where three girls beat the shit out of me, stole all my clothes and money, and left me bleeding in the Middle of Fucking Nowhere, Iceland? Yeah, that story. Part two's a real riot.

chapter eight

Miles Away to Vivian Girl

June 8 12:22 PM

Okay. I'm back.

I will say this in my defense: I could tell they were talking about me. All day. Even if you can't understand the language, a not-so-subtle point and whisper is easy to decipher. At first, I kept trying to be positive about it, but that went downhill pretty fast.

Maybe they think I'm cute? Maybe they want to know what my shirt says? Maybe they want to know what I'm saying? Maybe there's something on my face? Maybe I'm boring. Or just a bit uncultured? Maybe they think my dick is laughably small. I bet she's telling her friend how much I suck at oral sex. They're laughing at me. I know they are.

I didn't think—because I'd been trying so hard not to think—that they might be whispering to each other about you. About me. About me and you. And why not? It makes sense, right? You had a million and one blog followers all over the world. Some of your writings had gone viral. The *Mixtape* book was in Reykjavik, and Frankie had recognized it. The damn court case made headlines worldwide. Why wouldn't we be known in Canada and France, too?

Queers, gender rebels, feminists, activists, artists. I was reminded of you at every turn, but I kept pushing you out of the picture.

Have fun. Let go. As if I can just turn a key, press a button, and an elevator will shoot me above all this.

This part of the story is harder to tell.

I was a little drunk, but I remember what happened pretty clearly. Frankie and the brunette got out of the pool first. They put their clothes on and went into the changing room for a short while. I saw them grab the cans of paint out of my backpack, so I figured they were just tagging the place (and, technically, they were). I stayed in the water, floating next to the peacock girl. We'd found the spot where the hot springs trickle in, so we were warm and cozy, buzzed. She kept trying to float on her back, and even though I'd already proven myself a lousy lover, she didn't seem to mind me watching her. And when I swam over to help her, placing my hands under her back and holding her up so she didn't sink, she smiled up at me.

We were in that dusky late-night Icelandic sun, warm and drunk. I was holding her, that rainbow feather tattoo resting in the palms of my hands. Just me and a nameless French girl, her perfect breasts like little mountain peaks rising out of the water. Light as a feather, stiff as a . . . ha. You fill in the blanks. I don't know. I guess it's important for me to say that I was having a good time right then. I liked that she let me hold her. Keep her afloat. If someone were to ask me what I thought of her, I'd have to say she was a nice girl. Even now.

"Miles!" Frankie's voice echoed out through the valley. "Come look at this!" She was standing at the doorway of that filthy changing room, waving me toward her. The peacock girl skimmed away from me, and I got up out of the water, pulling my boxers on (thankfully, my boner had retreated at that point). I paused at the doorway to pull your boots on so I didn't have to step in all that ick, but Frankie grabbed my arm and pulled me inside before I could even take them down from the hook.

"Frankie! Jesus! This floor is gross!" The sensation of sticky brown goo seeping between my toes really brought out my not-so-masculine side.

"Just come here. We want to show you this."

I took two more steps inside. They lured me. That'd be the correct word for this.

I saw your name first. That was what stood out. On the side wall, under one of the windows, someone had used the can of Barbie/lipstick/labia pink to write *C'est pour Vivian.*

I didn't need Google Translate to tell me I was screwed.

Frankie hit me with a brick. I think it came from the wall of the pool. White, rectangular cement. I found it later on the floor.

My head rang like a bell. One moment I was standing, and the next I was in the muck, getting the crap kicked out of me. Ribs. Stomach. Junk. Both of them kept on kicking me, and my head was so fucked that I couldn't really do anything but curl into a ball and try to protect my more sensitive parts.

I've never actually been in a fight before. That's not to say that people didn't bully me. They definitely did. And I'm not proud of it, but I could be a real cruel kid to anybody that gave me shit about being fat or having two moms. I found ways to exact my revenge that left darker bruises than my fists ever could. Anyway, I can tell you that these two girls understand both methods. They kicked my ass and destroyed (what was left of) my soul.

I could hear the peacock girl in the doorway, pleading for the other two to stop. At least, that's what I've chosen to believe she was saying. I really don't know. Maybe she was goading them on. But I have decided that she stopped them and maybe even saved my life. They quit kicking and ran off. Left me in the mud and ick.

But not before grabbing my backpack (the one with all my freshly laundered clothes). My jeans (with my wallet and phone in the pockets).

And your oxblood Doc Martens (the only thing of yours I'd brought on this trip). I can still see them dangling from Frankie's fingertips as she ran. That's what hurt more than anything. More than a brick to the head or a kick in the balls.

One more piece of you slipping away.

Battle wounds are as follows: one black eye, two stomped testicles, several bruised ribs, and one gnarly-looking gash on my temple that probably needs stitches and will probably leave a scar. Do you think I will look sexy with a scar? I can pull that shit off, right?

I wonder. Did they attack me because I didn't save you from trying to commit suicide? Or is it because I dropped out of the court case? Don't get me wrong. I deserve it either way. I failed you. Twice. Someone shoulda kicked my ass a long time ago. Hell, I'm not even mad. I get it. I just need to know if more bad karma is coming my way.

Though, now that I think about it, I did have a little bit of luck. Help came in the form of a robot. No, make that TWO robots. Óskar is as much a clever little machine as the artificial intelligence in my cell phone AND twice as useful.

Anyway, I'd say I probably lay on that disgusting floor for at least half an hour. I threw up, 'cause that's what you do when someone smacks you with a brick, then kicks you in the balls. I'm not going to go on too much about that, though. I'm not trying to make you feel sorry for me. It was bad, but I never lost consciousness. At least, I don't think I did. And I got up eventually. I got up.

I went outside, and of course it was still fucking daylight. Or maybe the sun had set and risen again. Who the hell knows around here? I wandered for a little bit, unsure of what to do next. I found my Tourist T-shirt still next to the pool —they hadn't grabbed that when they stole my pants. I was so dirty that I didn't want to put it on, though. So, I got back in the pool and washed all the mud and goo off myself and my underwear. Carefully washed my head wound. Hopefully the water was clean enough. The blood had clotted, but when I rinsed, it started bleeding again. So, I ended up applying my warm, dry shirt to the gash on my head. Bloodied up my T-shirt. Fitting, really. You ARE a tourist, Miles. Bewildered and gullible.

The French girls had left their cooler (too heavy for them to lug in their grand escape, I suppose). I drank the last beer. Are you supposed to drink when you have a head wound? Eh, probably not. There were also two containers of *skyr* inside, which I gobbled up without a spoon. Just tilted my head back and chugged them down. Then I immediately went into survival mode, thinking, *Wait! Shouldn't I have rationed that food?* Because I was a pretty long way away from civilization. I remembered seeing a few houses scattered along the countryside, but the nearest one . . . How far of a walk is a twenty-minute drive? Fuck.

I knew my best bet was to get to a road. Start walking, or hope a kind stranger was willing to pick up a wet, bloody, half-naked hitchhiker who stank of muck and Viking booze. So I headed uphill, away from the pool. And probably three hundred feet out, I found my cell phone. It must have fallen out of my pants pocket when one of the French girls ran away.

Great news, right? Except that the screen was cracked and blank. And I'd left it on airplane mode. Great. Fucking. News.

I tried everything I knew about resetting cell phones, but the display was toast. The phone still worked—I could feel that "haptic feedback" vibration whenever I touched the screen. I could even get it unlocked, because I knew where the keys would be. But I couldn't really call anywhere. Who would I even call? I guess I could have called Mamochka, but then she'd have cried and panicked, and I'd have cried and panicked, and where would that have gotten us? Plus, like I said, my phone was on airplane mode. Emergencies only— to keep me from accruing ridiculous international roaming charges.

And there I was. An actual goddamn emergency. *Cue "No Phone" by Cake.* But then I thought, *Siri! Siri doesn't need buttons. Siri will save me!* Puuuush. *Dingding!* Then . . . nothing. No computer voice asking me what the hell I wanted. Yep. Siri needs internet to work, too.

So, I sat there and figured out how to turn off airplane mode without looking at the screen. I know that doesn't sound like a grand ordeal, but it was, trust me. Like, maybe . . . a forty-five-minute ordeal? Lots of complicated steps, but eventually I heard that *dingding* and said, "Call Hotel Skógur in Reykjavik, Iceland," and Siri said, "Calling Hotel Skógur." And I nearly wept with joy.

A guy picked up, and I immediately thought he was Óskar, but he told me Óskar was off for the weekend. Then I just sort of launched into "Look, I'm fucking lost and I really don't care how much this is going to cost me I just need someone to come pick me up, oh and can you please bring some pants?" He asked where I was, and I was like, "Uh . . . Iceland's oldest swimming pool?" He goes, "Selojakjmodnonajondkull" or whatever, and I was like, ". . . Yeah, that's probably it." He said he'd send someone, and I said I'd be waiting by the road.

So, I finished the rest of the walk up the hill. It took me, like, thirty minutes because, well, my balls hurt, okay? I figured whoever was coming to pick me up was coming from Reykjavik and so they'd be at least another hour, so I wasn't paying much attention when an enormous white Jeep with huge tires pulled up alongside me.

"Hello, handsome. How much for a blowjob?" The driver smirked at me, and I saw my own pitiful reflection in his mirrored aviators. Shivering and bruised. Pathetic. No wonder some strange asshole wanted to mess with me. Any other day I would have cursed this dude's mother and started listing off a few inanimate objects with which he could fornicate, but I was beat. Physically and mentally. So, when he slid out of the Jeep and walked toward me, I actually flinched.

Then I realized how little he was. And how blond. Óskar. Minus the man-bun. His hair was down, loose around his shoulders, and he was dressed sort of . . . I don't know, grungy? T-shirt and jeans, baggy cardigan. Very Kurt Cobain. My mushy brain couldn't make sense of him out of uniform and out of context. Plus, did he just make a joke?

"How did you get here so fast?"

"I was nearby," he said, looking me all over. I don't think he'd noticed how beat up I was until then. I felt very small and very naked. "Do you need to see a doctor?"

I shook my head and drew my arms up around my shoulders. Óskar was kind of the last person I wanted to see because I still thought he might be a smug little shit that my mommy had elected to babysit for me. And I was still a little mad that he'd mocked me in front of Shannon for rarely leaving the hotel.

But at the same time, he was looking very much like my knight in shining sport utility vehicle.

"I don't want to talk about it. Can you please take me back to Rey—to the hotel?" I got a little flustered, thinking he might laugh and leave me on the side of the road if I managed to pronounce his precious capital city incorrectly.

He turned and motioned for me to follow him back to his giant monster truck. We got in, and he reached into the back seat and handed me a neatly folded square of fabric. It was a pair of black and white plaid pajama pants. I pulled them on without a word, and he smirked at me some more while he started up the engine.

"The hotel called me to pick you up because I was nearby, but this is a little inconvenient. I will see to it that you have a bed tonight, but I cannot take you back to Reykjavik until tomorrow afternoon. I have some business to attend to. I promise not to ask you any questions if you will do the same for me." Big, blue-eyed-cat blink.

And thus began my very weird night with Óskar. Which I will tell you about. Later.

For now, we sleep.

chapter nine

Miles Away to Vivian Girl

June 8 6:02 PM

I did an impossible thing. You'd tease me so much—I just lied to Mamochka! I told her I fell while hiking. It was easier to lie via Skype, but still not entirely guilt-free. I think she believed me. I really just want to go home, but I don't want to worry them. Or waste money. So, I'll suck it up. I'm barricading myself in this hotel room again. More wound licking. At least the injuries are mostly external this time. God, I'm a wreck.

Miles Away to Vivian Girl

June 8 6:35 PM

Nothing's working. Nothing's changing. I feel like I'm being buried alive.

I hate labels, you know? I've been a lot of things, like the Son of Those Two Lesbians and the Only Queer Kid in School. How about That Guy Dating That Chick Who Used to Be a Dude?

The thing is, I'm fine with all of them (except for someone calling you a dude). For the most part, I've never been ashamed of my parents or my sexuality or you. Sure, there were times I wished things were simpler, that my life didn't leave me with so much explaining to do. It is what it is, and I can't really change any of that.

So it really sucks now to be stuck with this label because of a conscious choice that I made. I am now the Guy Who Threw Our Beloved Vivian to the Wolves. I don't know what to do or where to go from here. It feels like I need to apologize to the entire world.

And sometimes it feels like the entire world ought to apologize to me.

That's selfish. I know. But every once in a while, I get caught up in this fantasy where your parents show up at my door and tell me how wrong they were. I wonder, too, about all the trolls who filled your Haters inbox—do they know what happened to you? Would they take it back if they could?

I think about what I'd say if my mom apologized for not seeing the warning signs in you. Before I left, we kept having this same conversation. It's not even a conversation, really. She'd show up at the cabin or my bedroom or wherever I was trying to sleep and just talk at my face. Say things about how a lot of shit factors into a person's decision to commit suicide. That just because I yelled at you the night before doesn't mean it's all my fault. When she does that, it makes things worse somehow. It's almost like she thinks she has the power to absolve me. I wish she'd just be real. Say out loud that I screwed up. Admit that she did, too. Maybe then we'd be getting somewhere.

Miles Away to Vivian Girl
June 8 7:49 PM

Okay, I promised to tell you about Óskar. Two things first, so I can kind of set the scene. For starters, Óskar looks like a supermodel. That's not to say he's hot. You know how you sometimes see those angular, androgynous people in magazines and think, *How on earth did that awkward creature land a modeling contract?* That, in essence, is Óskar. He's perfectly symmetrical, physically flawless, and blond as all get-out, but sort of . . . alien? Then the light hits him just right and you go, *Oh shit, those are some gorgeous baby blues.* Or maybe I'm just really, really horny and everyone is starting to look damn sexy to me?

Anyway, the other thing is that his phone rang all night. Like, every ten or twenty minutes—and I'm not exaggerating. It kept vibrating in the cup holder between us—this old-ass flip phone, btw—and he'd snatch it up, look at the display, then set it back down unanswered. This happened from when he picked me up around one or two a.m. until we crashed. Not literally crashed. I mean, when we went to sleep.

So, back to where we were. Óskar had just picked me up from—and here is its actual name—Seljavallalaug, and I was . . . honestly, I was trying my damnedest not to cry. Not just because I was in pain, but just the idea of it. I'm still really upset, V. I've always been a part of the queer community, but turning my back on you meant turning my back on the rest of them, I guess. It's just really scary to know I won't be welcome anymore. The kids at Camp must be really mad at me too. Maybe not all of them, but enough for my parents to send me to the friggin' Arctic Circle.

Maybe that's why they didn't want me around. Maybe it wasn't for me to heal but to protect me from them.

I really regret letting everyone down, and for such selfish reasons.

Óskar turned the Jeep east, away from Reykjavik. I leaned on the window and watched the scenery, because the south coast is super pretty. There are really, really tall cliffs all along the road (none of those tiny baby mountains I'd seen leaving the airport). Green fields. Lots of sheep. And waterfalls pouring out of everywhere, like, every ten feet.

I decided the only way I was going keep my shit together was to not think about you, so I started getting really fixated on Óskar and his stupid phone. Since I was wounded and a little out of it, my mind wandered to some pretty weird places, and I ended up convincing myself that he was up to something illegal. I mean, he was driving to the middle of nowhere in the middle of the night. His phone going *buzz buzz* all urgent like he was late for an execution.

"So, are you, like, a drug dealer or something?" It was the first thing that came to mind.

"I can get you some weed when we get back to Reykjavik."

"No, man, that's not what I'm asking—"

"I said for you not to ask me anything."

"You are just acting all kinds of shady right now with your phone and your confidentiality clause, or whatever. If you're about to make me an accessory, I just wanna know, okay?"

He glared at me for an uncomfortably long time, then didn't say anything for the rest of the trip. He turned in to a long driveway with a squarish house at the end, maneuvering the Jeep behind a stone wall so that it was mostly out of view of the house. Weird house, black with white trim. It looked so ominous, even in the relentless Icelandic sunlight.

"You are in no danger," he said, turning to me.

"Uh, okay."

"But we cannot speak for the rest of the night." Bliiiiink.

"We can't?"

"No." He waved his hand dismissively. "We are going in that house—do you snorrh?"

"What? What does that mean?"

"When you sleep? Do you snorrh?"

"Snore? No, I don't snore."

He nodded. "Good. Then you can sleep. But no talking. Because I am not there. And you are definitely not there."

"No, I don't think either of us is all there right now."

"In the house."

"Yeah. Uh, we're in the driveway." Between my head wound and his weird accent, it was starting to seem like a game of Who's on First.

He blinked at me again and pointed a finger. "Quit fucking around. I know you understand me."

"Not really, man."

He paused for a second and scrunched up his face. "Did you ever sneak into a girl's room?"

"Ha. Oh, okay. Gotcha. Why didn't you say so?"

One more scowl, then he hopped out of the Jeep. He shut his car door very slowly and quietly, so I did the same. We took a roundabout way to the house, circumventing a huge red barn on our way to the back door. Óskar let us in with a key. We crept through a laundry room and up a flight of stairs. The house was old and sort of Victorian-looking on the inside. Floral wallpaper and scuffed wooden steps. In the middle of the upstairs hallway was a door with a word, a name I (correctly) assumed, painted on it. *Bryndis.* Óskar opened this door with yet another key, and we went inside. There must've been blackout curtains or something, because it took my eyes a second to adjust. I heard the lock click behind us and sensed Óskar moving about the room. He handed me this super soft knitted blanket and pointed to a chaise longue in the corner. I shuffled over to it and curled up, making sure to turn my head so that I didn't stain anything with my blood.

Even though I was in a strange house, uninvited, my

entire body relaxed when I lay down. I felt comfortable. And safe. At least I wasn't on the floor of some filthy changing room, getting an unsolicited spinal column adjustment.

Óskar pulled off his shoes and cardigan and crawled into the bed. There was a girl beside him, but I couldn't tell much about her other than that she was small, blond, and probably asleep. Óskar stretched out on his belly, facing away from her. I thought that was weird at the time. Why go to all the trouble to sneak into your girlfriend's house, then not even, like, cuddle with her? He just fell asleep. Pretty quickly, too.

His phone kept buzzing, and you know how light a sleeper I am. Plus, I was dealing with some PTSD shit, or whatever, and every time it went off, I'd twitch. Finally, I got up and grabbed it off the nightstand. The background on his phone was a photo of him and a blond girl. She was cute, grinning this big, sparkling grin. Óskar had on his usual serious face. The notification display said "27 missed calls from Jack." Well, it was in Icelandic, so it didn't exactly SAY that, but I could tell that's what it meant, because the name and the number were legible to me. There were text messages, too. I was so tempted to look at them, but I powered the phone down and put it back.

After that, I kept myself up worrying that I had a concussion and if I fell asleep, I might not wake up. I wasn't sure if that was a real concern or just something they put in movies. And then I was suddenly so exhausted that I didn't care. I wonder if that's what happened to you. Maybe you were just tired. Tired of being alive anymore. That's how I felt that night, so defeated that I didn't even care whether I'd wake up in the morning, or if I'd expire in a strange Icelandic girl's bedroom.

Óskar was sleeping a few feet away from me. His arms were bent up, hands tucked under the pillow. The shirt he had on was sleeveless, and his biceps were surprisingly buff. He looks like a fucking archangel when he's sleeping, and I was jealous that he had someone to wake up next to. I fell asleep, mildly pissed that he was probably the last thing I'd ever see.

Bryndis woke me up that morning. She's got the same supermodel looks as Óskar, but they work so much better on a girl. Resting her hand under my chin, she tilted my face, examining my wounds. It was the strangest thing in the world, to be awoken by some random but beautiful girl. And have her touch me so gently like that. I wanted to flinch away, embarrassed and taken aback. But I stayed still and let her look me over.

"Did you do this to him?" She glanced over her shoulder at Óskar. He was on her bed, laptop open in front of him and a mess of papers and binders and files fanned out around him. Schoolwork, I figured.

"No," he said, without looking up from his screen.

"Oh, are we allowed to talk now?" I asked.

"Quietly," he replied.

Bryndis told me her name and gave me a container of blueberry *skyr*. And a spoon! Such luxuries. Then she left for a minute and came back with a first aid kit. But while she was gone, I told Óskar his girlfriend was nice.

"Sister," he said, still focused on his computer. "She is fourteen. And if you try to fuck her, then I will fuck you. In the ass."

"A double date?" I said. "How delightful."

Bryndis returned and started patching up my face. She wiped the dried blood off me and put one of those butterfly things on the gash, then a big Band-Aid on top. And she gave me some aspirin, which I desperately needed. My head throbbed.

She told me I had striking eyes.

"Thanks. I'm sure you've heard that a few times yourself."

She smiled. *Fourteen*, I reminded myself. *Fourteen*.

She left again, whispering in Icelandic to Óskar. I was getting pretty tired of being gossiped about in foreign languages. Whatever she said didn't garner a response from Óskar.

"Hey," I said to him. "Can I use your computer for just a couple minutes? I need to cancel my stolen debit card."

He pointed to a desk in the corner. "Use hers."

I had a hell of a time getting around on Bryndis's little pink laptop. Everything was in Icelandic, plus it had a bunch of extra keys. I was able to get to my bank's website and report that my card had been stolen. I had to ask Óskar if I could receive mail at the hotel and what the address was. I could tell he hated being bothered, especially when he had to walk across the room and type the street name for me because I couldn't figure it out. But at least I've got a new card on the way. I had no clue what I'd do for clothes and food for the next seven to ten business days, though.

I started thinking about my wallet and what else I'd had inside. There was a photo of you—I hope those assholes saw that. It wasn't like I'd forgotten about you, if that's what they thought. And my driver's license (thank God I'd left my passport at the hotel). Thirty or forty American dollars. One of my three condoms. I'm over that now, though. No more following my dick around. Look where it's gotten me so far.

I shut Bryndis's laptop and curled up with the blanket again. The house was so still and quiet. Just Óskar tapping away on his keyboard and some muffled TV sounds coming from downstairs. I had about a million questions for Óskar, like when are we going back to the hotel and why did we sneak into your sister's bedroom last night, but, man, Óskar is weirdly intimidating for such a small, little dude. And I knew if I started looking for answers, he'd probably do the same: where are your clothes, and why are you all beat up? Eventually, the conversation would circle back around to you. I'm tired, Vivian, of defining myself in relation to you. I want to try just being Miles again, whoever the hell that guy is.

The morning dragged on. Mainly because I had nothing to do. Óskar eventually finished his work and loaded all his binders and shit into a big ol' man purse. Of course he has a trendy little satchel to match his trendy little bun. Though, to be fair, he was still wearing his hair down at the time.

(Yes, I know. I'm being shitty and sexist about Óskar's style choices. I think it's deep-rooted passive aggression from eighteen years of being raised to be the most accepting, PC guy on the planet. Damn, can I just be an asshole for a little while, okay?)

"My brother will be home soon. And then we will leave," he told me.

I was busy counting the stick-on plastic stars on Bryndis's ceiling for the third time. "Okay."

A few minutes later, we heard a crash from downstairs, like glass breaking. Óskar sat up, and then there was a little scream—Bryndis shrieking—and Óskar was gone from the room in a blink. I've never seen anyone move so fast in my life.

My stomach bottomed out then. My gut understood before the rest of me that something horrible was about to go down. Then, there was all this noise—crashing and pounding and screaming and shrieking. Chaos. It sounded like someone was getting murdered down there.

And I wanted to stay out of it. I'm not one of those brave souls running toward the disaster scene. In fact, when I heard bare feet slapping up the staircase, I had half a mind to hide under the bed.

Interesting fact I've heard about the Icelandic language: they don't really have a word for "please." Like, the phrase for ordering a beer would actually translate to "beer, thanks." So, when Bryndis appeared in her doorway and said (in English, of course), "Help. Me. Please," my blood went cold. She grabbed me by the arm and dragged me down the stairs into a little kitchen.

Óskar was beating the shit out of this naked old man.

Okay, the guy wasn't totally naked. He was wearing a robe, but it was open. Óskar was crouched over him, just whaling on the dude.

"Stop. Him," Bryndis said.

The image of Óskar's beefy little biceps flashed in my mind, and my recently kicked ass didn't want to tangle with him, but I also couldn't let him commit homicide. I tried to grab Óskar and pull him away, but he elbowed me hard in the gut. So, for my second attempt, I just threw myself on him, and we both tumbled to the ground. For a minute there, I was in between Óskar and the old man while they continued to scream what I can only assume were Icelandic obscenities at each other.

Then this other dude came into the kitchen. He was fortyish, ruddy complexion and ginger-haired, but with Óskar's and Bryndis's same ice-blue eyes. I kind of figured he might be their dad. And then he was shouting along with everyone else.

"He's American. He doesn't understand you!" Bryndis screamed at the new guy. I hadn't even realized he was talking to me.

"Get him out of this house," he said, pointing to Óskar and then the door.

I got up and pulled Óskar along. He didn't fight me too much, though he and his opponent were still shouting. We were halfway through the door when the old guy shouted something at Óskar that made us both cringe. *"Faggi!"*

"Keep walking," I said to Óskar, though I kind of wanted a shot at the old man myself. You know that kinda hate don't fly with me.

Outside, Óskar broke away from me and booked it to the barn. I followed him past the stalls of bleary-eyed sheep and up a ladder to the loft. I leaned on the window frame and looked out into the mountains. Óskar paced the floor, steam rolling out his ears. And then, like flipping a switch, he was fine. Calm again, as if nothing batshit crazy had just happened.

He squeezed in next to me at the window and pointed into the distance. "Wolcano."

"That's pretty close. Aren't you afraid it'll erupt?"

"It did. In 2010."

"That's the one, huh? With the impossible name?"

"Yes." He spewed out a name full of consonants and accent marks. "When I was a young man—"

"Pretty sure you still are one."

"I was afraid, yes. But that is a worry that only children have. When you first learn that something so consuming exists, you always imagine that it will swallow everything you know and love. But then you get older and you find out that all those horrible things you've imagined can happen anyway, no natural disasters required."

What a guy, huh? Still waters run deep.

Before I could comment on Óskar's musings, the ginger-haired guy showed up under the window with Óskar's bag thrown over his shoulder. We climbed down from the loft and then he and Óskar had a brief conversation without really looking at each other. Then the guy handed Óskar his bag, and Óskar and I went back to the Jeep.

On the drive back, I broke the confidentiality clause. I told him about Frankie and the French girls beating me up. I didn't say why. I hoped he assumed that it was a mugging. For now, anyway.

Then I went into sympathetic camp counselor mode and somehow managed to coax a few little details out of him. It turns out that the old man in the robe was Óskar's dad. He's got dementia now, and it's so bad that he doesn't recognize his kids. He likes Óskar's brother Karl (the ginger), but, for whatever reason, hates Óskar with a passion. And poor Bryndis looks so much like their dead mom that she can't be left alone with him. That was the scream we heard—Bryndis getting bent over the stove and groped by her own dad.

"I overreacted," Óskar told me. "But I would like for my sister not to lose her virginity to her father." He was really pissed at Karl for running off for the weekend with a girlfriend and leaving Bryndis to fend for herself. Óskar's been sneaking around the house while Karl's been away, trying to look out for his sister and keep out of sight of their dad.

"That's really fucked up," I said. "I'm sorry."

What I didn't say was that it was kind of nice to know that someone had a shit-ton more problems than me.

chapter ten

Miles Away to Vivian Girl

June 8 11:39 PM

When I got back to the hotel last night, I took a long shower, scrubbing all the mud and blood and ick off of me. I fell asleep immediately after, on top of my bed sheets. Later, I was awakened by the phone—Óskar telling me he'd be coming to see me in a few. I asked why, but he hung up without answering. So, I got up and threw on Óskar's PJ pants (which he had yet to reclaim) and a hotel robe while my Tourist T-shirt and one and only pair of undies soaked in the bathroom sink.

There was a knock, and I answered to find Óskar in the hallway. With a cop.

"Shit. What'd I do?"

Óskar handed me a mug of tea and stepped into the room, gesturing for the cop to follow. Once the door was shut behind them, he said, "Your debit card was stolen. Many banks won't reimburse your funds unless you file a police report. Also, you were assaulted."

I wanted to snark at him about the fact that he'd assaulted someone himself this weekend, but I just sighed and told the cop I wasn't interested in pressing charges. Before my card was deactivated, Frankie and the French girls had only managed to blow about eighty dollars, since nothing but gas stations were open on a Sunday. The cop was nice, though, polite and smiley. He sat in my desk chair and took notes while I laid the whole truth out. Well, I didn't mention the graffiti or oral sex, but other than that, I told it all. He didn't recognize your name, but when I mentioned your website, he said, "Yes, I have heard about that."

Hey, we're internationally famous, V. Canada, France, Iceland. Is there nowhere I can escape?

Óskar hovered by the doorway the whole time, sponging up the full glory of my plight. I wondered if he'd heard about you. What was his opinion on the matter?

The cop gave me a carbon copy of his report and a business card. I thanked him, shook his hand, and sent him on his way.

Before he left, Óskar said, "All of your clothing was stolen?"

"Yeah. I've got a new debit card on the way, but in the meantime I'm gonna need to hang on to your pants."

"Of course," he said, heading out the door.

"*Takk!*" I called after him.

After that, I went back to sleep, hard. Óskar woke me up again early this morning. "I have some things for you."

I let him in. He stood next to the television and unloaded a bunch of stuff from his messenger bag.

One black nylon wallet with an Icelandic flag embroidered on the front. "From our gift shop. Good souvenir. Check the inside."

A replacement bus pass. One prepaid debit card. "Twenty-seven thousand krónur—that's around two hundred dollars American. You can load more at the front desk anytime."

A pack of black and gray boxer briefs. A few pairs of white socks. A three-pack of plain black T-shirts. One pair of dark gray skinny jeans. "Everything's new except the trousers. They belonged to Atli. He's about your size, maybe?"

"Who's Atli?"

"Another concierge. Dark hair. Sometimes he can be quite loud. He said for you to keep them. He had them set aside to donate, anyway."

"Oh. Okay."

"I hope everything is to your liking. I've charged it all to your room, but if there's an item you don't want, I will refund you."

"No, it's fine. Great, actually. Thank you." My voice cracked ever so slightly. I hoped he wouldn't notice.

He glanced at me for a second, then stared out the window. "I should have taken you to the police Saturday night. And the hospital. I was selfish, too involved in my own affairs."

"It's fine," I whispered. I was overwhelmed. Touched that

someone had gone to so much trouble to take care of me. All at once, I missed Mamochka like crazy.

And I missed being able to look after you.

Óskar dug into his bag for one last item: a pair of raggedy black Chucks. "Maybe these will fit you? I'll need them back, though. They are frayed, but I'm fond of them."

He left the shoes by the corner of my bed and booked it out of there pretty quickly. I could tell he was the sort of guy that can't really handle it when other people cry—and I was clearly about to lose it. Especially when he gave me the shoes. I didn't want his shoes. I wanted your stupid fucking boots, and I was gutted all over again by the fact that I'd lost them.

I always tell myself I'm not going to cry over you anymore. And I always end up cocooned in my bed sheets, sobbing into my pillow. Fuck fuck fuck fuck fuck.

Miles Away to Vivian Girl

June 9 2:04 AM

Now that the floodgates are open, the wounds are fresh, and I'm not getting any sleep tonight, I might as well pull up one of my demons and look it straight in the face.

I've been thinking about the box, the money. The thing is, most people who intend to kill themselves do not make plans for the future. Many of them give their belongings away. They don't hoard thousands of dollars in a shoebox in the back of their closet. The fact that that shoebox exists means that, in some ways, an alternate reality exists. While there is no denying the fact that you willfully took a lethal dose of pills, I'm not so sure anymore that you actually intended to die.

This could be good news. God, I almost want to call your parents and spell it out for them. It's been speculated that they're keeping you on life support because, according to their religion, suicide is an unforgivable sin. Keeping you alive keeps you from eternal suffering, which is almost kind of touching, until you consider the fact that they care more for your "soul" than they ever did for you as a fully functioning human being.

Eternal salvation aside, the shoebox means something else: I think you intended for me to save you. You wanted to do what you loved to do: worry me. Terrify me. Have me beg and plead and bargain.

And I did all those things for you, babe. But I was too late.

Somewhere there's a parallel universe in which I went to check on you as soon as I got home that day. Or maybe one where we hadn't just had that stupid fight the night before. I envy that Miles in that universe, who still has the ability to kiss your eyelashes every night. Instead I'm stuck in this universe, being this Miles . . . this guy who is so goddamn lost without you.

I had stopped at the Redbox after school that day. I didn't find anything to rent. I also put gas in my car. I went home to Mom and Mamochka's for a while. Had a snack and watched some cartoons. I did everything I could think of to avoid heading back to the cabin with my tail between my legs. If I'd only been myself that day, not so stubborn, I'd have gone to your place right away for a cuddle and a chat, apologies all around. The doctors could never pinpoint what time exactly the brain damage occurred, only that it was a miracle I'd found you breathing at all. That's the American South for you — a doctor, a supposed man of science — doing his best to convince you that any alternative is better than death.

He was wrong. An unending coma is a thousand times worse than death.

I never told anyone, not even Mamochka, that there were several minutes there after I found you and after all the CPR I tried, when I just held your hand. Too afraid to call an ambulance because I knew how pissed you'd be if you woke up in a hospital gown, stripped, misgendered, and exposed.

Do you remember that time I tried to tell you the real story of "The Little Mermaid"? Not Ariel, but the original Hans Christian Andersen tale? You didn't believe me, so I drove to the library and found the book. It had a blue canvas cover with a gold-leaf mermaid on the front. So pretty — I took a photo of it with my phone. I read you the story, and you pouted, told me I'd ruined your childhood.

I'd laughed at the time, about the poor mermaid-turned-human who endlessly felt as though she were walking on knives. But that's what it feels like for me now. Every step without you brutal and terrifying.

Miles Away to Vivian Girl

Despite my sleepless night, I got out of bed early this morning. Still angry and hurt and tired, but I decided to put your memories away for a while. *Keep moving, Miles.* I put on the clothes Óskar had given me. The shirts are V-neck, a little more snug than I'm used to. I think it's that they are the right size for me now; I'm not wearing the same shirts that belonged to the me of two years ago. Same with the jeans. I've worn skinny jeans, but I've never been able to pull them off before. In fact, I look pretty good except for my black-and-blue face.

Óskar's shoes fit.

I had breakfast out in the sunlight. Toast, tea, and a boiled egg. Óskar wasn't at the front desk, but there was a dark-haired concierge. I checked his name tag—ATLI—then thanked him for the jeans. He gave me a fist bump. "Looking good!"

I felt a little less self-conscious about my black eyes.

I asked him where to shop for more clothes, and he showed me a few places on a map. "Clothing is expensive here. Don't look at the total. Just close your eyes and swipe," he said, mimicking a debit card swipe.

I handed him my prepaid card and had him load another two-hundred-ish dollars. Then I took the bus downtown and found a couple shops. I browsed for a bit, but as a guy who usually dresses in the effortless whatever's-on-the-clearance-rack-at-Hot-Topic style, I didn't know what to buy.

It was a big moment for me. Starting from scratch. I could actually reinvent myself. But I didn't know where to begin.

Eventually, I left my style choices to a shop girl with a lotus tattoo on her shoulder and aquamarine hair. I asked for two pairs of pants and a few more shirts. "Casual," I said, "but nice."

Business was slow, so she had plenty of time to shove me into the dressing room every two minutes, then give me a thorough inspection and commentary. Every so often, she glanced at my injuries, but she didn't ask about them, and I was glad.

"These," she said, handing me a nice pair of dress slacks. "You won't get laid Friday night unless you wear something a little fancy."

In the end, we decided on the dress pants and a pair of distressed (but not over-the-top) jeans. I also took her advice on shirts: button-ups, one red checkered flannel and a solid slate gray. She pointed out a striped sweatshirt and suggested I layer it over the flannel. I'd never have thought to mix patterns like that, but it worked.

I eyed a couple more things—a red velvet blazer and a pair of suspenders—but couldn't picture myself being comfortable wearing them back home.

"This, too." She picked out a slouchy gray beanie, which conceals enough of my messy hair to make it look decent.

I left the store with an armload of artfully wrapped packages and barely enough money left on my card for lunch. I had a salad ("no chicken, please") at a café and rode back to the hotel.

I planned to just dash back to my room and start sorting through my loot, but Óskar was at the front desk.

"*Halló.*"

"Hey."

"Everything go well for you today?"

"Yeah. Got some new clothes." I held up my armload of shopping bags.

He nodded and glanced down at the borrowed Chucks on my feet.

"Shit," I said. "I forgot to look for shoes."

"Not a problem. You can keep them for a few more days." He waved his hand, gesturing for me to come to the desk. "Come here."

The Jenga tower on his desk was freshly stacked and untouched. I slid a side piece out and plunked it down on top while Óskar grabbed a free city map from a pile next to his computer monitor. He unfolded it, circled an address, and pushed it across the desk to me.

"I know," I said, reading the name of the building he'd marked. It was the hostel where the French girls were staying.

"What do you know?" He chose a center block and pushed it through the Jenga tower. It landed with a thunk next to an artificial flower arrangement.

"That's where the French girls are."

Óskar looked like he wanted to strangle me. I took a step back.

"I spent all afternoon calling arrroundht to find this out for you," he growled, tapping his fingers on the map. "And, you know, this is the sort of information you should have passed on TO THE POLICE."

"I didn't ask for a cop, or for you to call around for me, did I?" I pulled another Jenga block.

"Silly me. I thought you might want your shit back." He flicked another piece from the tower.

"But you helped me replace most of it already."

Then he asked me if there was anything that couldn't be replaced. It was eerie the way he said it, like he knew how important your boots were, even though I hadn't really mentioned them to the cop. But how could he know?

Unless my theory about him gossiping with Mamochka is right.

And, well, damn. How am I going to explain to her and Mom that I lost your boots?

I stared at Óskar, and he stared back. We continued playing the most passive-aggressive game of Jenga in Icelandic/American history.

Óskar won, of course.

"My roommate speaks French," he said, sweeping spilled blocks into a smaller pile with his palms.

"So?"

"Do you want our help? Or should I just call the police and give them this address?"

"Are those my only two choices?"

He nodded.

"Fine, whatever. I hope your roommate is burly and twice as unsettling as you."

He blinked. "She can hold her own."

I sighed and gathered my shopping bags.

Óskar asked if I still had his spare elevator key. I said I did (thankfully, I'd tossed it on my nightstand before I went to the Laundromat). He told me to meet him on the roof tonight after he gets off work.

I'm so not looking forward to getting my ass kicked all over again.

chapter eleven

Miles Away to Vivian Girl

June 10 1:03 AM

Óskar was waiting for me in the creepy concrete stairwell with his roommate, who is this almost-six-foot-tall Megan Fox clone. She had that asymmetrical bob haircut, a black lace dress, and red, red lips. Surely this girl is some sort of Icelandic goddess and/or the end result of a couple thousand years of virgin-to-volcano sacrifice.

And, apparently, she was there to deliver me some weed.

"Oh, no, man. I can't." I busied myself with unlocking the door, then quickly shoved my hands back in my pockets so she couldn't hand the stash over to me. "I don't do that shit." Christ. I swear I don't know how I get myself into these situations.

Óskar looked annoyed. "But you asked me . . ."

"Yeah! Because of your constantly ringing phone, not because I was jonesin' or whatever."

"Fine, then." Óskar shoved the door to the roof open with his hip and threw an arm around his beautiful roommate. "We will have it without you."

I peered through the door, and again I was blinded by the sunlight flooding the stairwell. That rooftop is probably my favorite place in Iceland so far. So, I was really happy when Björk grabbed me by the wrist and pulled me along behind her.

Yes, Björk. That's her name. She hesitated when I asked, but Óskar just blurted it out.

She elbowed him in the chest. "Óskar! You told him my name!"

"Why can't I know your name?"

"Because," she said, plopping dramatically onto the lounger, "when I tell foreigners my name, I then have to have a long, boring conversation about the other Icelandic Björk. It's taxing. I tried going by my initials, BJ, for a while, but Óskar teased me. He's such a dirty old man."

"I hate when you call me that," Óskar said with a scowl. "I'm only two months older than you."

"Still a pervert," Björk whispered to me. She patted the space next to her, waving me over with her other hand. I grinned and sat next to her. She grabbed my left arm and started examining my matryoshka tattoos. "Beautiful."

I told her about how one of my moms was from Russia, so the three dolls were her, Mom, and me. Then we talked for a second about the fact that I have two moms, but it wasn't annoying. I kind of got lost, actually, in a moment that felt very intimate and sincere. Björk is just one of those people who know how to hold a conversation. She's like you.

She's the buffer. The perfect translator between Awkward Óskar and Miserable Miles. I liked her instantly.

While Björk and I were chatting, Óskar was getting comfy. He stripped off his tie and work shirt, and untucked the T-shirt he had on underneath. Óskar in that T-shirt amused the hell out of me, but I didn't say anything. It was pale green, with a picture of an angry-looking ice cream cone, and it said DON'T MAKE ME LOSE MY SPRINKLES.

Óskar sat on the other side of Björk and dug the plastic bag of weed out of her purse. "It's been a while since we have done this, yeah?"

"Years," Björk said, squinting at him.

But judging by the fact that neither of them seemed to know how to roll a joint, I was pretty sure they hadn't done it at all.

"Give me that," I said. I started with a fresh paper and fixed them up. Then I talked Óskar through the complex art of toking up.

He coughed out his first drag. "I thought you didn't do this shit."

"I don't. I hung out with the stoners in high school, but never had the balls to really be one of them. Too afraid of disappointing my Mamochka. You know how she is . . ." I said, hoping he was distracted enough to forget to lie.

"I have no idea what you are talking about." He passed the joint to Björk, who took a puff and held it for a second before dissolving into a dainty little cough. The two of them acclimated quickly, though, and before long I was rolling them another from what little green stuff was left in the bag.

"Hey." Björk turned to me and put her hand on the back of my head. She took a drag and pulled me toward her, pressing her open mouth against mine. It wasn't a kiss. She exhaled.

And I couldn't help myself. I breathed her in.

And then one of us laughed. Probably me. Then we were both laughing and coughing, and the sexiness of the moment was gone.

"Do it again," I said, looking into her eyes. And she did, but we laughed again.

Björk gave Óskar the joint and crawled off the lounger. She spun away from us, all black lace and legs. I watched her peek out over the edge of the building and didn't worry one bit about whether or not she might try to jump off.

And I thought, *Whose life is this?*

Beside me, Óskar sucked down a lungful of smoke. And then we accidentally made eye contact, and I could tell we were both thinking the same thing—about me shotgunning the smoke from Björk and whether or not it'd be acceptable to do that with him. He raised an eyebrow, almost like an invitation, like a dare. I didn't move. I still can't read him yet, not enough to know when he's joking. Just because a person's dad calls him a faggot doesn't mean it's true.

But I honestly can't say I didn't feel a little bit of electricity between us.

Static cling, hopefully. I'm not sure what I'll do if I actually have a crush on Óskar.

And then Óskar laughed, a little "ha!" with no smile to it as he sighed out the smoke.

"Feeling brave?" he asked me later. "Ready to go face your enemies?"

I'd been hoping the pot would make him forget about that.

We took the bus downtown because, thankfully, Óskar knew he was too stoned to drive.

And there I was in my usual role as Only Guy Stupid Enough to Stay Sober.

"How were you born? Were you adopted?" Björk asked on the bus, patting my knee.

"Nooo," I said. "Were you named after THE Björk?"

She smiled and pushed her bangs out of her eyes. "Icelanders use the same few thousand names over and over again, so there are many, many Björks."

"Are there many, many Óskars?" I asked.

"There is only one Óskar," His Royal Blondness said somberly. He was standing in front of our seats, keeping his balance with the bus pole in the crook of his elbow.

"I believe that," I said, and Óskar glanced away from me.

"I was conceived by two loving parents," I told Björk, "and a turkey baster."

She cackled. "People actually do that?"

I shrugged. "Dunno. I never asked for all the gory details. It's icky enough knowing that my uncle is also my dad. I mean, different side of the family. I may be from Missouri, but I'm not inbred."

Björk smiled and asked me—in Russian—if I spoke any Russian.

I shook my head, feeling like a bad son. "I know a few curse words. Some lullabies."

"Do you know how to say 'I love you'?" Óskar asked.

"Ya lyublyu tebya."

"Then that is all you need," he said.

When we got off the bus, Óskar and I looked left, toward the hostel, but Björk turned right toward a sushi place. "Can we eat first?"

"This one only eats plant matter," Óskar said, nodding toward me.

"Yeah. Not a fan of sushi. There's only, like, three kinds of sushi I can eat, and it all tastes like salt and oceanic decay."

"You don't like sushi?" Björk asked.

"Or coffee," I said.

Óskar cut Björk off before she could comment on that. "No food. We eat after we finish this task." Then he marched off toward the hostel.

The panic hit me like Frankie's brick as soon as we walked into the lobby. My bad day played over in my mind, and all I could think about was blood and pain, the stench of that changing-room floor. I veered into a side hallway and leaned against the wall, trying to catch my breath. Björk saw me flip out and followed me, but Óskar remained oblivious. I could hear him prattling on in Icelandic to the clerk at the desk while I pressed my forehead against the cool tile wall.

"Let's go outside." Björk looped her arm through mine and walked me back into the sunlight and fresh air. Somehow we ended up in a little garden. There were coral-colored poppies and twisty little bonsai trees. Bees and butterflies. Björk held my hand and showed me around, listing off all the plant names for me in Icelandic. Eventually I was breathing again.

"Thanks," I said, and we sat together on a concrete bench.

"Everything is a game to Óskar," she said. "It is best, sometimes, not to play along."

After a few minutes, Björk's phone rang. "We're in the garden around the corner," she said.

Óskar showed up empty-handed. "The French women have gone. They checked out this afternoon."

I nodded, thinking about your boots dangling from Frankie's fingers. Gone. Gone for good.

"I'm going back to the hotel," I told them, digging my bus pass out of my pocket. "Bye."

I thought Óskar and Björk might follow me, but neither

of them did. I closed my eyes on the bus ride, and except for the robotic voice spouting out unfamiliar street names, I felt like I was back in my own miserable life again.

I thought about what Björk had said about Óskar treating everything like it was a game. That straight face of his . . . I always wonder if he's messing with me, but I can never tell for sure. I'm starting to feel like one of his Jenga towers. Picked apart piece by piece. Waiting to crumble and fall.

Back in my room, all my new clothes were piled up on my bed. I started sorting through them, and I swear I got chills suddenly, almost as if someone were watching me. I get chills, in fact, thinking about it now. I looked up from my stack of new clothes, and there on the windowsill, like they'd just been there all along, was a pair of oxblood Doc Marten boots.

Not some brand-new replacement. Your. Boots. I could see the little dimple in the left toe from when I'd stepped on your foot the day after I bought them for you. You were so pissed that that little dent never came out.

YOUR BOOTS, V. Your fucking boots. Still tied together by the laces. I tiptoed over to them like they might skitter away from me again if I got too close. I touched the part of the sole that juts away from the toe. Lightly. Just a fingertip. Outside the window, the sky was all sunny and blue, and the light was filtering in just right. It looked like a painting, your red boots framed in blue curtains and sky. I grabbed the DSLR Mamochka had convinced me to pack and snapped a photo. It just seemed like a moment worthy of megapixels. Something I could try to capture, but still enjoy.

I breathed, and I could almost feel some of the horror slipping away. Your boots were back from wherever they'd been, only a little worse for the wear. Just a little black volcanic mud smudged on the sole.

And then, like some weirdo with a shoe fetish, I grabbed your boots and hugged them against my chest. I cried. For an incredibly long time.

chapter twelve

Miles Away to Vivian Girl

June 10 7:19 PM

I woke up this morning full of wants. No, desires. I was full of longing for things beyond my usual morning ritual of shower, self-stimulation, and breakfast buffet. It's funny how need works, isn't it? You're full and empty all at once. Full of this aching, itching, longing and empty in a way that can only be remedied by forward motion.

My black eye is healing. It's gone from violet to a hideous sickly yellow color. Ugly, but less noticeable from a distance. The gash is nicely scabbed up and is mostly concealed by my hair. Despite my messy face, the new clothes are doing wonders for my self-esteem. I couldn't wait to put them on. Today I went with the jeans, the beanie, the red flannel shirt. I tucked my pants legs into your boots and rolled up my sleeves. The reds and yellows and blues of my tattoos sync up nicely with the primary colors in the shirt. I messed with my hair and stared at myself in the mirror for a bit.

It's incredible how resilient the body is. After all I've been through—what a wreck I am on the inside—I somehow manage to look halfway decent. Some might say that, except for the black eye, I look better than before. I wonder what you'd say about me now, skinny and expertly dressed?

Aside from the desire to look nice, the thing that I want most that I haven't even been able to fully acknowledge until today, is to get my hands dirty. It's the sex I'm not having, yeah, but also the art I'm not making and the music I'm not listening to and photos I'm not taking and this beautiful country that I haven't even been looking at. A year and a half ago when my heart splattered on the floor, all this good shit fell out, and I haven't bothered putting it back in yet.

It took a literal ass kicking for me to realize that I deserve better things than I've been allowing myself.

And with that knowledge comes the desire to grab all that stuff up and load it back in. My head is still a swirl of ideas, and I'm not even sure where to begin.

That click of the camera yesterday felt good. Twisting the focus ring, manipulating light. It felt like a good first step, so this morning I tried it again. I draped my camera strap over a lamp, set the focus and self-timer. Then I crouched up on the windowsill and waited for the seconds to pass.

The light's shining from behind me in the photo. Me, in your red boots framed by blue curtains and sky. The sunshine was warm on my scalp, and all at once I couldn't stand my hotel room.

At breakfast, two more desires clambered up my shoulder blades and down my arms. I found myself desperately aching to capture the mountain view from my favorite table on the patio. I opened my iPad and brought up Sketch Club. Ignoring the gallery of doodles you and I had collaborated on so many nights lying in bed, I opened a new canvas and lost myself for a while, tracing the steepled mountaintops and spindly little trees in my line of sight. I wish I'd thought to bring a stylus, but I did okay with just my fingertips. It took only ten minutes for me to scribble up a messy landscape and siphon away enough tension for me to move on to my next task.

I took a peek at the Camp Vivian Facebook page. I decided going in that I was not allowed to make myself miserable over it. I would look, absorb, and carry on. No big emotions involved. Sure.

There are a handful of new faces, but it's the familiar ones that almost had me in tears. I swallowed my sobs and sat with my hand over my mouth, scrolling down the page. It looks like Tee's been made art director in your absence, a job that most likely would have fallen to me, had I stayed stateside this year. One of their projects caught my eye. I shut Facebook and Googled around until I found a tutorial and the address for a craft store in Reykjavik.

And that led me to my second desire: I had to find a way to thank Óskar. The laundry list of favors he'd done for me in the past week was nothing short of ridiculous. And I had a feeling that somehow he was responsible for locating your boots. I mean, how else?

Plus, it's not like I have any friends here. I don't know if Óskar is doing all this shit because of his job, or Mamochka, or general kindheartedness. The kindheartedness seems like a bit of a stretch. Not that he's hateful or anything . . . it's more like he normally exists on a level of professionalism that doesn't allow for human emotion to seep in. At least when he's not beating up his dad, anyway.

People like that tend to have a lot of interesting layers. I've seen his dark side, so I was kind of dying to see him smile about something. Not his curve-lipped customer service smile, either. A real one, using his whole mouth.

So, I went to the craft store for fabric paint. At a grocery store I found a bottle of bathroom cleaner with bleach in a spray bottle, a new toothbrush, and some rubber gloves. I also grabbed a free copy of the city arts paper to use as a drop cloth, then headed back to the hotel.

It was a messy project, and I didn't want to risk ruining hotel property. Plus, I figured the fumes might be bad. The elevator key was in my pants pocket from last night—I'd accidentally pocketed it instead of returning it to Óskar. So, I went up to the rooftop and spent the next couple hours turning two of the plain black shirts Óskar'd gotten me into DIY galaxy tees. One for him. One for me.

It's pretty simple, really. You twist and swirl the fabric, then spritz it with bleach for the stars. After that, take an old toothbrush and use that to splatter blue and purple nebulas all about. I had no way of knowing if it'd be to Óskar's liking, but I personally thought it looked pretty damn cool. I used the hair dryer in my room to set the fabric paint, then washed them in the sink with a little body wash to get rid of that bleach smell.

I hung mine up to dry, but Óskar's got the hair dryer again. That was the longest part of the whole process—getting the damn thing dry enough to give to him. I had a gift bag and tissue paper from my clothing parcels yesterday, so I put the shirt, his pajama pants, and Chucks inside, then headed down to the lobby.

Atli and a girl were at the front desk, huddled over the Jenga blocks. I asked for Óskar, and the girl walked me to an office around the corner. When I knocked, Óskar said something in Icelandic. I leaned on the door and spouted out a couple sentences I'd learned by poking around on an online translator: "I don't speak Icelandic. Except for that sentence and this one explaining it." Sure, it's kind of a rip-off of a *Family Guy* joke, but I heard a short, genuine "Ha!" as Óskar opened the door.

"Your pronunciation is terrible," he said, gesturing me in. "Come in here, American boy. I have treasures from your home world."

"You seem like you're in a good mood—hey, are those Subway cookies?" I said when he offered me a familiar white paper bag. "Treasures from my home world, huh?"

I have seen several Subway restaurants in Reykjavik. Domino's Pizza, too.

I took an oatmeal raisin and sank into a cushy chair in the corner. "Gawd, this does taste like home. Sorry to interrupt your dinner." There was a half-eaten sandwich on his desk.

"It is not a problem. I could use a break from the paper-work," he said, closing a couple tabs of spreadsheets on his desktop. All of his binders and shit were spread out, too. So I guess what I had once thought was homework was work-work. I wonder how old he is.

Also on the desk was a framed photo of Bryndis, Karl, and their dad.

"Wait," I said. "Is this your office? Are you the manager of this hotel?"

He nodded, bringing up a browser tab. "Look, one more thing for you."

Netflix. He fucking pulled up Netflix like it was no big deal.

"How?!"

"Techy computer stuff. You have to create a private net-work and treeeK your computer into thinking it is in the States."

"Huh."

"What do you want to watch?" he asked. "Bring your chair here so you can see more closely."

"Oscar?" Shit, I said his name wrong. But he didn't cor-rect me.

"Yes?"

"I'm going to hug you."

"No!" He tried to shrink away.

"Too late!" I crept up behind his chair, threw my arms around his skinny little shoulders, and dropped the gift bag into his lap.

He ignored my brief embrace and focused on the bag. "What's this?"

"Your shoes and pants. And I made you a gift."

"Takk." His ears had turned red. He unwrapped the shirt. "You did this? It's very cool. I like it."

"Do you?"

"Yes." He was still a little flushed, which is weird. I imagine with his job people probably bring him gifts all the time.

"Okay. Well, I just wanted to say thanks for everything. Particularly the boots."

"Boots?" he said, picking at his sub. "What boots? Wasn't me. Must have been the elves."

"Elves! I'm not falling for that we-all-believe-in-elves stuff, man. I think your nation as a whole got drunk one Christmas Eve and said, 'You know what we should all do to mess with people . . . ?'"

Óskar scoffed. "You shouldn't offend the *huldufólk* like that. They are always listening. Quite intelligent creatures —clever enough to know that three cash-strapped, transient women would have little use for a pair of men's boots. All they had to do, I'm sure, was to get up early in the morning and check the two or three resale shops downtown—"

"Ah. So they found my boots before you decided we should go all vigilante on the people who stole them?" What was that about? If he found my boots early yesterday morning, that meant he already had them when we went out last night. Did he just need to get me out of the hotel so he could have one of his co-workers sneak the boots into my room?

"Oh, I don't know. I don't always communicate well with elves. But I do believe they also may have hacked our computer systems so that they could charge your room for a rather large finder's fee. Clever creatures."

"Hmm. That IS clever. I guess I'll have to make a few tiny little galaxy shirts and leave them out in my room like that old shoemaker fairy tale."

"That would be wise." He turned back to his computer. "Do you like *It's Always Sunny*?"

"Uh, yeah!"

So we watched an episode while Óskar finished off his sandwich and moved on to the cookies. I laughed out loud a couple of times, but the most Óskar ever did was a little scoff every now and then. After the show was over, he told me he had to get back to his paperwork.

"Well, wait. I have to talk to you about something. And it is work-related." I leaned my elbow on his desk, as if what I was about to say was all very casual.

Óskar wadded up his trash and tossed it in the bin under his desk. "Is something the matter with your room?"

"No. The room is good. I'm sick of it now, though."

"You want a different room? They all look quite the same, I'm afraid."

"Nah. I just want out of it. I guess I need you to do your concierge stuff, or whatever." I sighed. "I've been thinking about my purpose. The purpose of my trip, I mean."

"Yeah?"

"I'm here because I lost someone. I mean, you heard me telling the cop about what's been going on with my girlfriend, right? And I need to, like, process, I guess? Um, she was kinda my first love."

That's how I've decided to start thinking of you. Lost. First. Love. It's poetic, but also kind of . . . normal? Lots of people lose their first love. Maybe everyone.

"I'm sorry," Óskar said.

"No, I'm sorry. I don't mean to unload all my neurotic shit on you. I'll just say that I'm trying to figure out how to let her go, but, also I want to do something to honor her. I started something, and I don't really know where I'm going with it." I told him about the photos I've been taking. "Her boots are really important to me. So, thanks."

Óskar sat up a little straighter in his chair. He was doodling on a yellow legal pad, and he wasn't looking at me, like he was trying to give off the impression that he didn't care. But I'm starting to think that maybe Óskar acting uninterested means just the opposite.

I've never met anyone so benevolently shifty before.

He glanced up. Brief eye contact, and his voice was really

soft. He knew he was venturing into rocky territory. "What was she like?"

I hesitated, because I wasn't sure I wanted to go there, either. He nodded and went back to his legal pad. He was drawing a spiral, or a labyrinth, maybe. A maze.

"She was electric. She was really extroverted and outspoken and emotional. Just really alive. That's why it sucks so much to see her in a hospital bed. All these tubes and machines, man. The sound." I imitated the Darth Vader noise of your respirator. "That's it. Just this awful, inhuman sound."

Poor guy didn't know what he was getting himself into. It was like once I had given myself permission to talk about you, I just couldn't stop. I did a sudden 180, switching subjects from Hospital Vivian to the girl once who seemed more superhero than human. "I fell in love with her at a music festival. My best friend, Brian, was supposed to go with me, but he ended up having to bail, so Vivian bought his ticket. And she changed the whole experience for me. Like when me and Bri go to a show, we usually just chill out in the back. But V's one of those people who pushes her way through the crowd. And she dances and gets really drunk. She talks to strangers and makes friends. She did mushrooms one night and wandered off, scared the shit out of me, but I honestly don't know if I was worried about her, or just chickenshit about being alone. So when she finally showed up at our tent that night, I freaked out on her. And she was like, 'You finally like me.' Because I guess she'd had a crush on me for a really long time. And then she kissed me."

Óskar kind of almost smiled at that. His maze had spread out, covering a quarter of the paper. I felt like I was in that drawing of his, and I'd somehow blocked myself in. But my walls were made of words, and I didn't know how to find the end of the story anymore.

What if I do something with those photos? Share them somehow? Will people like them? Will they be disgusted, think I'm riding your coattails or somehow profiting from what happened to you? And if you, the strongest, most incredible person I've known, couldn't handle the trolls, how will I?

"She kissed you." Óskar's voice brought me back to the story I was trying to tell. "And then what?"

"And that kind of freaked me out. Because this whole sexuality thing has always been kind of wonky for me. Like, it's hard being a mostly straight guy in a really gay environment. Sometimes I just need to escape that bubble. And other times, I feel like I have to project 'gay' just to fit in, which is sort of the opposite problem that most people in my life have. There have been long stretches in my life where I've been like, 'Nope, I'm straight, totally straight, la la la,' and all that. But, like, right now, I'd say I'm queer. Technically, pansexual. And if you want to get really accurate, demisexual, maybe. But I just like 'queer' because it's sort of old-fashioned and hilarious."

I paused to see if any of that jargon was making sense to Óskar. But, as usual, his face was a blank slate. I still have no clue where he sits on the Kinsey scale.

"But, anyway, Vivian always seemed very sure of herself in that respect. Like even when her parents didn't agree, she was still adamantly screaming, 'I'm a girl. I like boys.' She was an activist, and she made this huge, amazing website. She just knew how to make ripples, you know?" I said. "Like, if I toss something out there, it'd just stick to a wall. V could make stuff bounce. She was really creative, and she liked to document everything. I helped her with that—like I helped her brainstorm and filmed her YouTube videos and worked on her site design—stuff like that. She was getting pretty internet famous, especially with other queer kids, but I wasn't really into that aspect so much. I'm a behind-the-scenes kind of guy, you know?"

Óskar nodded. Maybe I hadn't lost him yet. His labyrinth wandered toward the far corners of the page.

"Um, I guess you could say that we fought fairly often, but that's not something I want to focus on, or anything. But it does sort of say something about our relationship. I mean, she drove me up the wall sometimes, but I loved her so much that the good outweighed the bad. But now I'm sort of buried in the bad, and she's not here to dig me out. So, yeah . . . sorry. I just said a lot. And nothing at all, somehow."

Óskar raised his eyebrows. When he realized I was finally

done blathering, he blinked a few more times and said, "It's interesting. And I think your intentions are noble."

I didn't feel very noble, but I just nodded along. "Vivian's website is gone, and that's pretty much my fault. I don't think I could ever make anything as good as *Mixtape* on my own, but I want to do something. For her. For, like, closure. Does that give you a better idea of my purpose? I mean, do you think you can help me with that?"

"I will figure something out. Could I have some time, maybe, to think on it?"

"Oh, yeah. Okay."

"Thank you again for the shirt."

"No problem." I got a little flustered then, like I had done something wrong or wasted his time. I knew I'd said too much, and I couldn't take it back. So I just got up and headed for the door before my mouth could get the best of me again.

As I was leaving, Óskar ripped the maze he'd been drawing out of the legal pad and handed it over to me. Along the bottom, he'd written the word *hinsegin*. I just looked it up. Icelandic for "queer."

No clue if he's mocking me. Or maybe just giving me another obscure term to throw around. Or, I guess he could be telling me something about himself.

No clue.

He called my room a few hours later. "Check youhrr email." Click, dial tone.

From: oskar@skogarhotel.is

Miles,

I think that Vivian would say that the best way to honor her life is to cherish yours. Do you think she would tease you for sleeping the day away in your hotel room when you are in the most beautiful country on earth? If she were here with you, wouldn't her boots have already traipsed across black sand, over mossy lava fields, and behind waterfalls? I trust that you would have followed dutifully along, ensuring that all her favorite moments were captured on film or carefully jotted down. Once, perhaps, you might have believed that your life was best lived in the shadow of hers. I hope that it is not too forward of me to say that that is no longer the case. Your purpose, like that of any young man traveling alone in a foreign place, is to find yourself.

For starters, I would say that you should see more of Iceland. Have I not mentioned that this is the most beautiful place on earth? Get plenty of rest tonight and be in the lobby tomorrow at 8:45. I have booked you a tour, if you're so inclined. It is a long tour. You will be gone most of the day, but there are plenty of sights to be seen. I would like to tell you more, but I think you might enjoy a surprise. The cost is around $70, and you are welcome to decline if it does not interest you.

I was thinking about Vivian's love for documenting,

your need to help her, and of wise American expres-
sions. It's clear you already know that the photos you
have been taking are important, and I agree that you
should share them, even if it frightens you. I've taken
the liberty of creating an Instagram account for you,
so that you can document your own journey. A fresh
start, and nothing too intensive. I am not a counselor,
but I would recommend that you use this as a catalyst,
a way of moving from helping Vivian tell her stories
to living your own. The account name is miles.in.her.
shoes, and the password is your initials plus your
room number at the hotel.

Well, those are my ideas for now. Please let me
know if you feel they are silly and stupid, and I will try
to come up with something else. Hopefully I'll see you
in the morning. Oh, and be sure to dress in layers, as
the weather here can be quite unpredictable.

Sincerely,

Óskar

chapter thirteen

Miles Away to Vivian Girl

June 11 11:15 PM

I took, like, a thousand photos today. But I also made sure to look at things outside my lens. I'm trying to find a good balance here, between making art and living it.

I love having all these photographs, though. When I finish up this message to you, I'm going to load them onto my iPad and tinker for a while. I might set up the Instagram and even post a few of them. I haven't decided yet.

I wore my galaxy shirt today. It would have been weird if I'd showed up in the lobby and Óskar was wearing his, but obviously when I saw him, he was dressed for work—shirts, slacks, bow tie. He was busy at the desk, but when he got free, he came out to the patio and sat across from me during breakfast.

"Are you going to eat zhat?"

"That was the plan." But I slid my plate forward. He

grabbed a slice of pineapple and bit in. I asked what his deal was with stolen food, and he said it just tasted better. Then he gave me my voucher for the tour—South Shore Adventure, it said. I told him I wasn't sure about the Instagram, though. "I'm still trying to decide if this constant need for megapixels is detrimental to the human experience, or whatever. But, as you can see, I have this big honkin' camera around my neck . . ."

He moved on to a piece of banana bread and didn't offer any opinions on the matter. I asked him if I could take his picture and he said, "Absolutely not," so I didn't, but now I'm dying to.

The tour was really nice. I was on a bus a lot of the day. Everyone around me seemed to be a couple, and there I was next to an unoccupied seat. So there was this underlying tinge of loneliness all day, but I just shoved it aside as best I could.

I wish I could tell you every little detail, but there aren't words. I walked on a glacier, a black sand beach, behind a waterfall. I stood at the base of a nine-hundred-foot waterfall, then sprinted up a staircase and looked out over the top. I browsed the folk museum, went inside a turf house, and listened to a ninety-four-year-old man play the organ inside one of those boxy little Icelandic churches.

The tour guide said that elves are myth from Christianity —Eve's unwashed children that she tried to hide during a surprise visit from God. Lately I don't know where I stand on this whole religion thing, but when I was in that church I kept thinking about how Óskar locating your boots sort of felt like a miracle to me.

Every time we stopped to see a landmark, I'd try to divide my time. I devoted three quarters of it to "me time," just sponging up all the things that I needed to experience. The other quarter I'd spend photographing your boots. A few people from the tour group asked me why I kept taking off my shoes. I felt a little awkward, but decided to play the mysterious artist and told them simply that it was "a project."

Each time I missed you, or thought the landscape was something you'd love to see, or when I started to imagine you there and began to frame a photo of you in my mind—I would snap a picture of your empty boots instead.

By the end of the day, my socks were soaked and black with volcanic ash and sand.

Miles Away to Vivian Girl

June 12 5:19 PM

This morning, while searching for a fresh memory card for my camera, I found that sketchbook my moms had given me before the trip. I took it with me to breakfast, stopping to borrow a pen from Óskar at the front desk.

He was on the phone when I saw him, so I just made a gesture like I was writing in the air and he sort of half smiled and plunked a whole coffee mug full of pens on the counter in front of me. Even though the pens were all the same, forest green with a tree and the hotel's logo on the side, I lingered over them, like choosing a particular one was difficult for me.

But, really, I was listening to Óskar speak English to someone on the phone.

"I haven't been ignoring you. Perhaps if you had scheduled this visit—No, I hate surprises. You should know that by now." He was speaking slowly, like the person on the other end was a kid on the verge of a tantrum. My guess is significant other. I tried to imagine what Óskar's slighted lover might look like, my mind cycling between some haughty European girl with one of those long cigarette holders to, perhaps, one of those old vaudeville weightlifters with the unitard and the tweedly mustache. No actual human being could fill that role, just a caricature who looked good in stripes.

Óskar finally plucked a pen out of the cup and handed it over with a look that suggested I be on my way, so I pocketed the pen and cruised off to the breakfast buffet. I've got this whole thing down pat now. First thing I do is make my tea. A white porcelain cup filled to the brim from the hot water dispenser and a bag of Earl Grey from the basket sitting on the bar. Let that steep while I load up my plate. This morning, though, I grabbed a second, smaller plate and loaded it up with fruit and cinnamon bread.

Then I slid the extra plate into the spot across from me and waited for the fairies to arrive.

"Uh-uh-uh. That's for the hidden folk," I said when the Breakfast Thief showed up. "You know, the ones who retrieved my shoes."

"I think fairies eat only icicles," Óskar said, munching on a strawberry. "Or honeysuckle dew."

This is going to sound weird, but Óskar, like, has this silence that comes with him. He's like that moment at the movie theater, right when the lights first dim. It's a hush that demands attention but doesn't expect anything in return.

I finished my plate and sipped my tea. Óskar took a butter knife to his food, slicing the grapes in half and dicing the bread into smaller and smaller squares. There was no sound except the clinking of silverware and some birds overhead. It's a rare thing, I think, to find someone you can really talk to. And even more rare to meet someone whose silence complements your own.

After a while, I cracked my sketchbook open—literally cracked because the spine does make such a lovely noise. I sat, pen in hand, but I didn't know where to begin.

So I pushed the book across the table and offered Óskar the pen. He started drawing lines, another labyrinth, but just along the edges of the page, creating a frame. He left the center blank and passed it back to me.

"What does this say?" I asked, pointing out the foreign words he'd woven into the maze.

"If you find yourself lost in a forest in Iceland, stand up."

I looked past him to the landscape surrounding the hotel, where the trees are so small and sparse. "Right on."

After breakfast, I walked downtown and took the elevator to the top of that big church that's in all the travel brochures. I spent some time looking out over the city, sketching those colorful rooftops that Mamochka had shown to me. I used the same page Óskar had started, so my drawing was inside of his.

It's not at all how I thought it'd be. All this art I'm slowly making without you. I thought the actual act would bother me, the drawings, the photos. But they aren't the problem. Getting started is the hard part. That second before the shutter snaps. Or the distance between the pen and the page.

I'm closing those gaps now. And it feels pretty good.

While I was up there sketching, the bell in the tower rang. Noon. It was the loudest sound in the world, something that jostled my whole body. I felt hollow, then filled with sound. It shook me, V. Maybe even woke me up.

After I left the church, I went to the craft store again and got some of those nice, inky watercolor pencils. I think I might want to try filling that drawing in sometime.

Then I walked around for a while, took a few more photos of your boots. I like the city. I think I'm getting a good feel for it. It might be time to leave. To go bigger. Get out.

I'm thinking about renting a car sometime and just driving out along the countryside. The thing is, I don't want to do it by myself. Who road-trips alone?

Miles Away to Vivian Girl

Earlier I was sitting on my bed, eating dry cereal and watching bad Icelandic music videos, when Óskar showed up at my door. "Put your shoes on. We're going for a beer run."

"Well, look at you. You look like the fuckin' sixth Ramone." He had on jeans, a white T-shirt, black leather jacket, and his Chucks. Also, a nose ring. And his hair was down. Friday Evening Óskar is very different from Rest of the Week Óskar.

"Shoes," he said, like an impatient parent. Then, "There were only four Ramones."

"Riff Randell was the honorary fifth Ramone," I said, lacing up my boots. "Not to mention the other real members that came and went throughout the years."

On the way to his Jeep, Óskar asked me if I knew a lot about music, or just the Ramones. And he also asked if I'd heard much from his favorite band, R.E.M. Interesting choice.

"They're the Smiths of the American South," he said.

"I'm from the South. Sorta," I said.

"Me too. South Iceland."

I laughed. He zipped out of Reykjavik and onto the road toward the airport. When I asked why we didn't just get booze in the city, he told me his cousin works in one of the shops at the airport and would sell us the alcohol duty-free. I still don't fully understand what "duty-free" means, but I guess it makes things a hell of a lot cheaper. Also, there's a limit on how much alcohol one person can buy, so that was why he was dragging me along. Not that I minded, but . . .

"What's the, uh, drinking age here?"

"Twenty."

"I'm too young, man."

"Really? You look older."

"I didn't get carded on the boat the other night," I said. "Must be my old soul."

I'd brought my camera with me. After I snapped a couple shots of the lava fields out the window, Óskar pulled over and said I should try walking on the moss.

"But don't be an asshole," he said. "Any damage you do takes decades to heal."

"I'm not an asshole. I'll be gentle with your precious moss."

We crossed the street and climbed up the hill to the lava field. It was glorious, spongy and soft, like walking on a trampoline. Or the moon. Óskar said the US government sent the astronauts to Iceland in the 1960s to study the lava fields in anticipation of the moon landing. Very cool.

He watched me photograph your boots against that green alien landscape and said nothing in his Óskaresque way. And when I was done, he asked if I wanted him to take my picture. I don't know why, but I hesitated for a minute, then handed the camera over.

I gazed out at the little baby mountains while he snapped my photo. I felt so self-conscious. Then I thought *screw it* and laid myself out in the moss, which was kind of what I'd been wanting to do all along. It's inviting stuff. So soft.

Óskar raised his eyebrows and snapped another pic. Then I got up and dusted off, and he gave me my camera back before we headed to the car. He crossed the road ahead of me, and I ended up having to wait for a bus to pass. While I waited, I took a photo of him walking away from me in long strides. The highway is really close to the shore in that area and the angle of the photo kind of made it look like Óskar was wandering off into the ocean. It's a really cool picture, but I was afraid to show it to him.

"Are you going out tonight?" he asked. "You have to do the *rúntur* at least once. Some of the pubs are all ages."

"Yeah, probably." I hadn't thought about the barhopping tradition since my night with Shannon.

We talked for a little bit about the tour he'd sent me on. I thanked him again, told him I was getting closer to figuring out . . . whatever it is that I'm supposed to be figuring out.

"So, are you going to sleep with my roommate?" he asked when we pulled into the airport.

"What makes you think that's on my to-do list?"

"How old are you?"

"Eighteen."

"No eighteen-year-old man goes alone to a foreign country for a month without intending to get laid."

"Might as well sample the local fare." I grinned and

shrugged, as if getting some action would not be a life-changing experience.

"Lucky for you, Björk will be at the *rúntur* tonight. She's an artist too, you know? And she is a little freaky. We once went to an orgy together, she and I. We didn't fuck anyone, though. Nobody was using condoms. I guess it makes sense. Who has time for condoms in an orgy? But, we had both recently finished reading *Just Kids*, and we figured we were the next Patti and Robert—though, I am not sure who is Patti and who is Robert, since she is the artist and I am the musician. But neither of us wants to die of AIDS, so we left."

Besides his volcano speech, that is literally the most Óskar has ever said to me, and I love that it was about orgies and Patti Smith and condoms and shit. Seriously??? This guy, Vivian . . .

"So, what? Did she, like, say something about me?" I asked. "I mean, what brought this up?"

"Yeah, she think's you're cute."

"Cute? Is that the exact word she used? Not, like, 'ruggedly handsome' or 'panty-dropping' or anything?"

"I don't know. Maybe *cute* isn't the right word. She said it in Icelandic. At any rate, suffice it to mean she probably wants to sleep with you."

Hello, world. I'm banging Björk in Iceland tonight.

"I'll bring condoms," I offered. Derp.

"Good idea."

So, we went inside the airport, and Óskar bought ALL THE BOOZE, then we headed back to Óskar's apartment in Reykjavik to drop it off. I was kind of hoping to see Björk again, but Óskar told me she was working.

"This place is hella swanky, man." Hardwood floors, slanted ceilings, and all fancy modern furniture. A grand piano in the living room.

"I'm moving sometime," he said, with his back to me as he stocked the fridge. "It doesn't suit me anymore."

"No, it suits you perfectly. It's all nice and composed at first glance, but somewhere . . ." I turned and bolted down the hallway. "Somewhere around here, there's got to be a really messy bedroom!"

"No!" Óskar chased me down the hall.

There were three doors in the hallway. I skipped the first one, figuring someone as guarded as Óskar wouldn't choose the bedroom closest to the living room. The next door was either the other bedroom or a bathroom, but I decided on the latter, heading for the third. Óskar beat me, skidding ahead and blocking me so that his back was to the door.

We were standing really close. Practically chest to chest. And there it was again, that stupid electric jolt of attraction. I could feel something else from him, too. A boundary that I wasn't allowed to cross.

"Huh," I said. "You hiding a body in there?"

"A painting. I didn't want it to catch you off-guard."

Whatever sexy electric body chemistry I'd been feeling instantly turned to lead, and my stomach churned. I could think of only one reason why Óskar'd be concerned that a painting might throw me for a loop. I swallowed hard and pushed past him, into his bedroom. It was tidier than I'd figured. The bed was made, and all the furniture matched. He had a few guitars hanging on the wall.

No skeletons in the closet. Just one of your paintings hanging over his bed.

"Well, fuck."

He plopped down on the corner of his mattress while I went in for a closer look. So, I guess Óskar is the proud owner of a print of *Winged Embrace*. Now that I think about it, I do remember Mamochka telling me that one of them had sold to someone in Iceland, a seemingly insignificant detail that had slipped my mind until it hit me in the face. How was I to know that I'd someday be standing in that person's bedroom staring up at this painting of me and you wrapped in each other's arms?

"You know what's funny? I always think of these things as hers—Vivian's paintings. But looking at it . . . I designed her wings. I made them out of an old bed sheet from the thrift store—I even used a sewing machine. And my horns —cardboard and craft foam. I posed us and took the inspiration photo. Hell, even . . . Look, see those green brushstrokes right there in the background? I did that, too. There is so much of me in this painting, and it's so fucking weird that it's in your bedroom. Goddamn, why am I looking at this right now? What the fuck?" How could he have this painting, this piece of me—of us? Seeing it made me almost certain my mothers had had a hand in this somehow. Did Mamochka bribe Óskar with a painting in exchange for looking after my sorry ass? The beer run suddenly felt manufactured, and that kind of stung.

I shot Óskar a glance and waited for him to concoct the perfect lie. Which, of course, he did.

"I got it a year ago, during the fundraiser for Vivian. It was a gift to me from my boyfriend. My hopefully-soon-to-be-ex-boyfriend. He's a collector of LGBT art and artists. He found the print online, and I liked it. I like Henry Darger, and Vivian's story touched me, so he bought it for me. He buys everything I want. It sickens me."

I frowned and decided to let the subject of the conversation drift to him instead of me. I still felt unsettled by the painting, but to be honest, I was intrigued. I mean, even if my theory is true and he IS babysitting me, it's sort of fascinating to wonder why someone like him would ever agree to that. I mean, does he like our art that much, or what?

"So you have a sugar daddy, huh? I wasn't even sure you were gay."

"You can't tell?"

"I . . . maybe? I dunno. I think my gaydar got damaged on the plane. All you Scandinavian hipster types seem pretty queer to me. Anyway, you have this nice guy buying you shit all the time, and you're sick of it?"

"I don't feel comfortable discussing my relationship problems with you." The way Óskar can just shut down and shut me out is almost a visible, tangible thing. He's so damn weird and interesting that I just want to, like, hold him upside down and shake him. See what kind of cool stuff falls out.

"You have a practically nude portrait of me and my now-comatose girlfriend hanging over your bed, and you . . ." I trailed off because Óskar himself had trailed off, out of the room and down the hall. I took one last, long look at the painting. I had forgotten about the prints. Since I destroyed the original, it makes me feel a little better knowing at least a few copies exist somewhere out in the world.

Anyway, I'm back at the hotel now. I took the bus because I could kind of tell Óskar was done dealing with me for the day. But before I left, he gave me a six-pack of Viking beer and told me to start drinking it around midnight and not to even think about leaving my room until I'd finished the whole thing.

I told him I wasn't much of a drinker. I wasn't even sure if I could drink that much by myself.

"Then you don't deserve to be in Iceland," he said.

"So, when and where should I meet you and Björk?"

"We'll run into each other eventually, I'm sure. If not, you'll find someone else to take home tonight. It's the *rúntur*; everyone gets laid. Have fun."

So, yeah. Sitting here waiting for the clock to turn. I'm about to crack open that first beer.

Whatever happens tonight, I'm sorry and I love you.

Miles Away to Vivian Girl

June 12 11:03 PM

One beer down. That wasn't so bad. Blehhh. Good God, that website Brian sent me to is just the worst. Super misogynistic. I'm trying not to let these "scoring tactics" infiltrate my brain too much. If Björk wants to sleep with me, okay. I'll give it a shot. But I'm not going to play her.

Right now I'm thinking about that conversation you and I had on our first official date. We were in a mostly empty theater watching some action movie, something that was all machines and explosions, interspersed with flashes of female nudity. Neither of us was really into it. I mean, I like breasts and bombs if I'm in the right mood for them. But that first-date awkwardness was really sinking into me.

You too, I guess. You turned to me and whispered, "I'm not going to have sex with you."

And then I inhaled a kernel of popcorn and almost hacked up a lung trying to clear my airways. You gave me your soda when I slurped on mine and found it was only ice. Anyway, once I could speak again, I said, all suave, "Good, 'cause I was really hoping we'd go get some fro-yo after this instead."

"I meant ever. Not just tonight. Ever," you said, every word a quick little jab, like you were throwing knives.

"Okay," I said. Maybe not the right response. I said it quickly and thoughtlessly because something needed to be said. A few minutes passed, you and me watching shrapnel fly across the screen.

"Sorry. It's just that your mom told me that the best time to talk about sex is when you're not already in bed, you know? I felt like I needed to get that out there as soon as possible, because I don't want to mislead you. Do you want to talk about it some more?" That two-year age gap between us really made a difference back then. I hadn't quite wrapped my brain around the possibility of us actually having sex sometime (to be fair, I thought about it constantly, in that abstract way a lot of teenage boys do), and there you were being honest and open, prepared. For all your goofiness, you always knew how and when to be mature. "Do you have any questions for me?"

"Nope."

More silence. Well, except for that awful movie.

"Okay. Well, I think you should say more. It feels like you're not processing what I'm saying. Like, you're not acknowledging me."

I glanced over at you. You had a red bandanna around your hair, like one of those old-timey biker girls. You looked damn cute. "I think you're just trying to scare me away. 'Cause that would be easier, right? Better to be rejected right from the start than to get your hopes up, huh?"

Then you laughed this tense laugh and said, "You sound just like your mother."

I shrugged, reaching for your hand. Your fingers slipped through mine, and everything felt a thousand times more electric and intense. "Mom told me to read up, so I'd sort of know what to expect. It's, um, dysphoria, right? Or is it that you don't feel that kind of attraction at all?"

"Dysphoria. Yeah. The feels are there, but I don't like to see myself naked or let other people see me naked. I thought it would get easier, but lately it's just been worse."

"Listen, let's not worry about it right now. I'm not trying to dismiss what you're saying, but I also think we should go into this with, like, a clean slate, right? We'll just see how we feel as things progress."

God, I do sound like my mother.

You smiled and thanked me for being so considerate and sweet. But now I cringe at what a snake I was. I'm like one of those creeps from that site Brian sent me to. You told me how you felt, and I tried to convince us both you'd change your mind. I still worry. And I'll never truly know if pressing you to work through your issues actually made things better or worse.

Hell of a thing to get worked up about right before I'm supposed to go out and party tonight.

chapter fourteen

Miles Away to Vivian Girl

June 13 2:18 PM

So, something happened. It happened in that way everything's been happening lately: unexpectedly, awkwardly. Sort of horribly.

Let's see. I choked down about three and a half beers before calling it quits. I think I'd like beer if it didn't, you know, taste like shit. At least I was feeling a little buzzed by the time I got downtown. It was around one a.m., and at first the streets were kind of empty, but then it seemed like the whole world decided to show up at once. People poured out of buses and parked their cars just sort of randomly wherever they could fit. Then everything was loud and colorful. I did what everybody else seemed to be doing, wandering from bar to bar. Hands in my pockets. I was wearing my nice gray button-down shirt, and it didn't make me look too out of place. I still felt it though, this notion that I was a small person inside a big machine. That any moment, the world might swallow me whole. I wished I'd listened to Óskar and finished off that six-pack, because I was too self-conscious to talk to anybody.

Eventually I ended up in the coolest place—a *Big Lebowski* bar/bowling alley. Everyone was drinking White Russians and quoting lines from the movie, laughing too loudly. I did talk to some guys there. Just straight guys, dudes from Arizona. General chitchat about what a weird little place Iceland is. But, hey, at least I didn't have to worry about those frat boy types giving me shit about you. I didn't stay very long, though. It was too hot and crowded in there for me to do my wallflowering.

A little later, I was just standing on the sidewalk when this Icelandic girl started talking to me. She was drunk and friendly, but not really my type, so I was glad when the rest of her group came and collected her. I was a little flattered that someone had noticed me.

I was terrifically bored after only an hour and a half. Sleepy, too. I started fantasizing about my bed, but then I thought—no, fuck no, Miles, you are not going back to that bed alone tonight! So, I went farther down the street.

One of the things that kind of helped me, oddly enough, was thinking about you. You'd like this, this late-night sunlit Reykjavik. It's the sort of thing you'd gush about in your blog, every moment captured in sexy, sparkling photographs. You're the kind of girl who'd fit in just fine on a *rúntur*. I could almost see you, gliding along those brick streets, your silver glittery dress turning all the Icelandic boys' heads. They'd never notice me, the guy with the camera, always three steps behind. They'd laugh at your jokes, but never hear me feeding you all my best punch lines.

So, take you out of the equation. And the camera. Just Miles, the *rúntur,* and some alcohol.

Experiences. Genuine human interaction. Memories over megapixels. That's what I was shooting for, anyway.

Easier said than done.

I saw a couple gay bars, but I didn't go in. I went in some shitty all-ages dance club full of spray-tanned blond girls . . . and ended up letting myself get shuffled to the fringes again.

"*Haaaalló,* American boy." Then, suddenly, Óskar was there in his Ramones getup, flanked by Björk, who'd borrowed his leather jacket. She was much taller than him in her high-heeled fuck-me shoes. Both of them were gorgeous in the blue bar light, fashionably sparkling with that hazy sheen of sweat they'd earned on the dance floor.

"Hello, Icelandic dude." I was really happy to see him. Just to finally have someone familiar to talk to.

He squinted and leaned close, raising his voice so I could hear him over all that bass. "We've seen you three times already, but we weren't drunk enough to speak with you."

I didn't know how to respond to that. Am I so lame that no sober Icelander would dare speak to me in public? I decided to ignore it. I just grinned and said hi to Björk, and she grinned back.

Just then, a dark-haired man in an expensive suit arrived with three drinks triangled between his hands. He was ridiculously handsome . . . sort of Christian Bale–ish, maybe? Even before he pressed one of the cups into Óskar's hand and said (in an adorable British accent), "Sorry, love. There was quite a queue at the bar," I could tell he was Óskar's moneybags boyfriend. He handed the second cup to Björk, then took a sip of his own.

"This is Yak," Óskar said, nodding toward him.

"Yak?" I asked. "As in the woodland creature?" I raised my hands up by my forehead, fanning my fingers into antlers.

"As in Jack," the British guy said.

Ah, Jack of the Twenty-Seven Phone Calls. I already didn't like him.

"Even though 'Oh-skargh' insists on having his own name pronounced correctly," Jack continued, "he can't be bothered to return the favor."

"Oh?" I raised my eyebrow and turned to Óskar. "You know, I'm not sure I've ever heard you say my name before. How do you say Miles?"

Then Óskar looked me right in the eye and said, so completely deadpan that I almost missed the joke entirely, "Kilometers."

I paused for a beat, then the gears finally turned and I laughed out loud. For the first time ever, I think, Óskar genuinely smiled at me. I understand why he keeps that thing tucked away. Óskar's smile is just awful. All gums. Horsey.

But I'm glad he smiled at me.

Right after that, Björk squealed over the song that started playing, and she dragged me away to dance. And you know I normally get bored or self-conscious after about thirty seconds of dancing, but Björk had on these tight, shiny pants, and the way she moved in them, close and tipsy and warm, made me forget about everything else for a while. Maybe my problem with dancing is that I overthink it. With the right partner, and the right amount of alcohol, it can actually be a pretty simple thing.

While I was trying to have fun dancing with Björk, though, I caught myself sort of visually checking on Óskar and Jack. Maybe it's just because Óskar told me he wanted to break up with Jack, but those two seemed pretty unhappy. Sometimes I'd look over and see them arguing, and then a few minutes later, they'd be making out in some dark corner booth. Honestly, I just kind of felt sorry for them—that sort of relationship seems exhausting.

The more I saw of the Jack and Óskar show, the less appealing the thought of having a relationship seemed to me. And I don't mean with Óskar. I mean with anybody. It's too much trouble, too much risk, to give yourself to someone completely.

Even if I can be a pretty good boyfriend. I mean, I was, wasn't I?

But, anyway. Last night, I thought, *Fuck all that ooey-gooey relationship shit. I just need to be an animal for a while.*

I danced with Björk some more, and quickly moved along to making out. I put my hands in her hair, my tongue in her mouth. I held her against me and occasionally kissed her against the wall. These were different kisses than I've had before. Stranger kisses. Shallow, I guess.

It scared me a little, the way I let myself get lost.

And then Óskar was there, leaning on the wall beside us, doing that thing where you exaggeratedly clear your throat. "Sorry to interrupt. Yak's in a mood, and he wants us to leave."

"Let him," Björk said, staring into my eyes as she mussed up my hair. "You can stay out with us."

"Or," Óskar said, directing a rare moment of eye contact my way, "perhaps we could all go home? Plenty of alcohol for all of us there."

I thought I could probably use some more liquid courage. And it'd be a good idea to be close to a bed or a bathroom because I was starting to figure my night would end with me laid out in one or the other, so I said, "Yeah, BOOZE. Let's do that."

Outside it was still daylight, all four of us squinting and groaning as we stepped out onto the sidewalk. Jack lit a cigarette and led the way back to the apartment. It was a really short walk. I hadn't realized how close they lived to downtown.

So, a lot of the night was Óskar and Björk coercing me to "dreeenk mohr." Ugh. But, drink I did, tossing back everything they handed me until I was stoopid, incoherent drunk.

"You're keeping up better than I expected," Óskar said. "You can almost dreeenk like an Icelander."

"He's Russian," Björk said. "I think they invented wodka."

"That was the Polish," Jack corrected.

Óskar poured another round of shots, and we all said, "*Skál*," which is basically Icelandic for "cheers."

"I have definitely, definitely, definitely never been this sloshed before," I said.

"Sloshed," Óskar repeated, trying out the word. "I like that."

"You're welcome."

And then he smiled again, and even though Björk was all nestled up with me and Óskar's stupid sexypants rich boyfriend was stretched out on the couch, I couldn't stop myself from telling him he should smile more often.

That's not even something I would normally say. I hate when people tell others to smile. Damn wodka.

"I should get to bed," Óskar said, rising to his feet. He dragged his boyfriend off the couch, and the two of them hobbled off down the hall draped in each other's arms.

That left me and Björk. She either didn't notice my slip-up with Óskar or didn't care. We made out some more and then she said, "Do you want to go to the bedroom?"

I started to get a little nervous, despite my dangerously

high blood alcohol content. And, as you know, when I get nervous, I have to piss. So, I excused myself and fumbled my way into the bathroom. I, um, may or may not have peed sitting down because I was too damn wobbly to do it otherwise without making a mess. After I zipped my pants, I ended up leaning there against the bathroom wall. I knew exactly what was waiting outside that bathroom door. And it paralyzed me.

"Are you okay, Miles?" She pronounced my name like "My-else." Not "Kilometers."

"Uh-huh." I reached for the toilet and found out just how damn handy that giant flush button must be for this nation of perpetual binge drinkers.

"Are you getting sick?"

"No. No." I leaned, pressing my forehead against the door. That animal part of me retreated into the white-tiled cage of her bathroom. I was myself again, not at all sure I was cut out for this. "I'm nervous. I haven't been with anyone in an embarrassingly long time."

"That's okay."

"No. Nope. No, it's not."

"I'm coming in."

I leaned away from the door and ended up having to catch my balance by taking a seat on the edge of the tub.

Björk entered the bathroom in just her bra and underwear.

I just stared at her like a slack-jawed caveman. I've never been with someone that conventionally beautiful before.

"You still want to fuck?"

"Uh-huh."

She pushed her hair back behind her ears, knelt between my legs, and proceeded to give me the shortest blowjob of my life. Her life, too, I'm sure.

I cannot believe I'm saying this to you, V. I came in, like, two seconds. My dick betrayed me! It was just like, *Warm? Wet? DONE!*

"Shit. I am so sorry. Shit."

She leaned past me and spat into the bathtub while I tried to calculate how soon I could get to the airport and leave this godforsaken hellpit of shame and never look back.

To make matters worse, I could feel her shoulders shaking as she laughed silently.

"Jesus. I'm going to go now. Time to curl up and die." But I couldn't quite find my balance.

"No. Stay." She got up on her knees and pushed my hair out of my face. "I'm sorry I laughed. But it is a little funny, right? A little bit?"

I closed my eyes and bit my lip, but a small cough of a laugh still got out. "Yeah."

And then she said—in language that, frankly, I feel pretty uncomfortable repeating to you—that since we'd gotten that part out of the way, if I could get going for her again, I'd surely have the stamina to do all the stuff that she wanted me to do to her. And then she grabbed me by the hair and asked me if I was still interested in doing that stuff to her . . . and I was like, "Uh, yes, ma'am?"

She led me into her bedroom and then we were making out and taking off my clothes and all that, but she stumbled a bit, and I started thinking about the c-word. Ha, not that c-word. The other one that my moms are always drilling into my head: *consent*. We'd both had way too much to drink for this to be cool, but it felt good, and I didn't want to stop kissing her. And I felt guilty that I'd gotten off and she hadn't.

So, I kept fooling around with her, but I kept asking her if she was sure a lot.

Until finally she was like, "Are YOU sure?"

"No." My underwear was still hooked around my left ankle, and I pulled it up and on before I could change my mind. I started babbling, trying to explain myself, but I was really, really drunk. And I could feel the anxiety starting to claw at me the way it has been lately. So I just apologized and shut my stupid mouth.

"It's all right," she said.

So I lay there on her bed in pitch-darkness for a bit, waiting for my heart rate to slow down. I thought about the other day when she walked me around the park and soothed my nerves somehow. I said, "Will you show me your bedroom?"

"You'll think I'm strange."

"I like strange."

Björk flicked on the lights. She pulled on an oversized T-shirt and gave me a little tour of her bedroom. "I'm studying to be a hair stylist and special effects artist. It's for practice, you know?"

Her walls were pale purple, and there were shelves and shelves of dolls all over the place. Turns out she likes rescuing old ugly dolls from thrift shops and modifying them. Some of them were chipped and gruesome, straight-up horrifying. Others she'd turned into fairies and mermaids and snake-haired gorgons. She had a little worktable in the corner, too. Tools and paintbrushes and stuff.

Óskar'd said she was an artist, hadn't he? He said something about how he was a musician and she was an artist, but I hadn't asked about either because I'd been too focused on the promise of sex.

"They're brilliant," I said.

Then she laughed. "Most boys that see them worry I'm a serial killer."

"Nope. I get it. I'm way fluent in artsy weirdness, too."

So we just hung out and talked art. She told me about the dolls and the art school she attended. I told her about *Mixtape* and this new Instagram thing.

I should have known. God, I should have known from the start that I wasn't really looking for a hookup after all. I just needed someone else to listen to me get all angsty about you and art.

Eventually, I guess we both fell asleep. I woke up on her

bed next to her, both of us curled up on top of her covers. A couple hours had passed, and I had to piss again. Still a little out of it, I managed to fumble my way to the bathroom. I was actually able to pee standing up that time. But then when I went to wash my hands, I caught a glimpse of myself in the mirror and nearly shit myself.

The left half of my face was gone. There was just a skull. I recoiled from my reflection, then immediately brought my face toward the glass again.

Paint. It was fucking paint. While I slept, Björk had made me up like a skeleton. Just on the one side of my face, leaving the right half of my face, and its fading bruises, untouched. It was an expert job—the way she made my eye sink deep into its socket and turned my lips into a row of exposed teeth. Scary and beautiful. I loved it.

I stepped out of the bathroom and quietly shut the door. What next?

Óskar and Jack were in the living room. They were huddled around the piano, Óskar on the bench, facing away from me, and Jack leaning against the side.

Also, they were very clearly wearing each other's underwear. And only each other's underwear. Óskar was in a baggy pair of plaid boxers, and Jack had somehow managed to stuff himself into a tiny pair of neon green briefs. There was something so weird and indecent about it, but I couldn't quite bring myself to look away.

Jack scowled at me. "Bloody hell, you look positively ghoulish."

"Too bad she didn't give me a haircut," I said. "I could have used that."

Óskar finally turned around and studied my face for a brief moment. Jack's hand slid across his back to the opposite shoulder.

Didn't he tell me they were going to break up?

Óskar didn't say anything. He just blinked at me, then turned back to the piano. I thought he might play something, but his fingertips barely grazed the keys.

"So, uh, what's the Icelandic etiquette here? Am I supposed to sleep over, or just drift back to my hotel?"

"Leave," Jack said.

But the Icelander said, "Stay."

So, I stayed.

Björk was awake when I returned, and she'd burrowed beneath her covers. I lay next to her and propped myself up on my elbow, hand resting on the unpainted side of my face. "Thanks."

She nodded and shut her eyes, tracing a finger down my chest.

"Do you ever get stuck?" I asked. "You know, like, artistically blocked? Where you want to make something, but you don't know where to go or what to do next?"

"Mm-hmm," she said. "Everyone does."

"Well, what do you do?"

"I find out what my muse is hungry for. And then we feast."

She was gone when I woke up again around nine. I lay there on her bed for a while, a little achy, but mostly in my heart. I whispered your name, feeling this strange and terrifying sensation of guilt and pride. And I guess Mom's right: I'm not processing. Because I didn't know what to do with those feelings. So, I got up, straightened my clothes and messy hair, then headed for the door.

It seemed like the whole house might have been empty, but Óskar popped up over the back of the couch as I was making my exit. He was wearing his galaxy T-shirt, and he had a big pair of headphones on.

"Want breakfast?"

"Nah. Food doesn't sound too appealing right now."

He pulled the headphones down around his neck and leaned forward, draping his arms over the back of the couch. "Did you have a good time last night?"

"Yeah. It was pretty cool."

He nodded.

"Where is everyone?" I asked.

"Björk's gone to work, and I sent Jack away."

"Away for good?"

"For milk. We ran out."

"Did you change your mind about breaking up with him?"

"No. I'm procrastinating. It's not simple."

"It's never simple."

"The man has his claws in nearly every aspect of my life. To walk away from him will be . . ." He scrunched up his nose. "Cataclysmic."

"Really? This from the guy who's not afraid of the volcano down the street?"

He just nodded again, and I could see the wall starting to come up.

"I guess I'll head out. Um, tell Björk she's welcome to come see me at the hotel sometime. I can't really do the whole phone number thing—"

"She won't want to see you again."

"Oh."

"It's nothing you did. That's just the way things are here. We don't really date or anything like that. Next weekend, you will find someone else to spend the night with. Sex is somewhat impersonal here."

"Oh, okay."

"She said you were good, though."

"Is that really what she said about me?" That girl is an angel.

"Yes." He lay back down on the couch. "In case I don't see you again, enjoy the rest of your trip."

"What? Why wouldn't you—"

"Because Jack owns the hotel. Just like he owns this flat and everything in it. But I can't let him continue to own me."

I left with my heart in my throat. Just the possibility of not seeing Óskar anymore . . . No. This is so stupid. I barely know him.

On the bus ride home, everyone stared at me, the half-drunk, half-skeleton boy. I didn't care. All I could think about was getting to my camera and photographing whatever was left of the paint on my face.

And I couldn't stop mulling over unspoken conversations in my head.

All these questions. I don't know how to tell an almost stranger that I need him. How can I expect him to keep taking care of me when he clearly has so much of his own shit to deal with? How do I tell someone I want him after I've spent the night with his roommate? Am I just projecting my need for a connection onto the first person who came along?

Or am I feeling something real?

chapter fifteen

Miles Away to Vivian Girl

June 13 9:43 PM

I did kind of a weird thing for a guy who spent the night before drinking and almost literally screwing around. I didn't shower or even change my clothes until a couple hours after I got back to the hotel. I was thinking about that time I bought a copy of *Wreck This Journal*, and you and I spent all autumn doing shit to that book. A few months ago, Mamochka got me another of Keri Smith's books, *How to be an Explorer of the World*. I really like that one a lot. It's full of all these prompts that are meant to change the way you interact with your environment. The key is to go deeper, to experience life with all your senses.

And last night was kind of like an experiment from *Explorer*. Or a page ripped from *Wreck This Body*. I'm not sure. But I got way the hell out of my comfort zone. I came back to this pristine hotel room, and I did not feel like myself. Or maybe it's more accurate to say that I was wearing layers and layers of last night all over my skin. The new clothes and the smudgy skull paint. I didn't smell like myself. I smelled like Björk's citrusy perfume. And beer. And sweat and sex.

I did take some photos of the skull paint. I went in the bathroom and sat in the dark, using just the illumination from my iPad to light up my face. The pictures are so eerie and lovely in a dark way. Some of the best stuff I've done in a long time.

And I like that they were a collaboration of sorts with this interesting Icelandic girl.

Anyway, so after the pictures, I kept myself wrapped up in all those layers, and I messaged you. Not sure if I was punishing myself or testing my pride. To determine that, I'd have to figure out if I'm okay with the fact I got wasted and fooled around with someone strange and new.

I guess that probably is something I need to figure out.

Okay. So, you'd be mad. There's no way around that. If you woke up right now and found out I'd been in some other girl's bed, you'd scream at me. And don't think, even for a second, that I haven't heard every word of it inside my own damn head today. I have. Believe me, I have.

But—and this is the important part—I am learning to separate my voice from yours.

It's over now, though. I've showered since then. I watched the gray water from the face paint circle the drain.

It's over, it's over, it's over. I changed my clothes. And now I find myself thinking about Óskar. A whole lot.

I'll get back to you on how I feel about that one.

Miles Away to Vivian Girl

It's Saturday. I spent a good chunk of time today wishing it weren't Saturday, that I could fast-forward through the weekend and find out if Óskar's going to be at work on Monday. Now that I'm aware of my crush on Óskar, I'm REALLY FREAKING AWARE of my crush on Óskar.

I'm counting the hours until I might see him again, and I'm counting the days until I never see him again.

That's the thing, isn't it? I keep thinking about the oranges on my doorknob and the clothes and all that stuff he did. And the way he blushed when I gave him the shirt. And even though he set me up with his roommate, I do think he's interested in me. But, like . . . how? Does he just want to hook up? I mean, that's pretty much all he'd get at this point. I'm headed home in sixteen days. Even if he wanted something a little deeper than casual sex (and he probably doesn't, right?) that really isn't possible for us.

Us. Goddamn. I just said "us," and it didn't mean "me and Vivian."

This feels dangerous. I'm setting myself up for more heartbreak, and I should just run the other way and cross all my fingers that I don't see him again.

But did I do that this afternoon? Nope. I went to his apartment.

I somehow managed to convince myself that this trip was to see Björk. I had a plan, actually. I told myself that I wanted to see her and let her know she was awesome for not tossing me out after I made a fool of myself on the edge of her bathtub last night. And I did have a couple other, non-Óskar-related ulterior motives.

That asshole Jack was sitting on their front stoop when I got there, smoking a cigarette and yakking on his cell phone.

I've taken to calling him That Asshole Jack, because that's what Björk calls him most of the time. And, knowing what I know now, it seems to fit.

Anyway, when I came up to the house, he sort of looked at me over his sunglasses like, *What the hell do you want?* then just waved his hand at the door like I should go in. So I did.

Björk was curled in an armchair, deeply engrossed in a book. She had glasses on and little purple shorts that really showed off the length of her legs. I stared at her for a moment just thinking, *Whoa, I coulda slept with that?* because she is really beautiful in a lead actress sort of way. She wouldn't be my first pick from a crowd, but most guys I know would be chomping at the bit.

"Uh, hi," I said.

She looked up from her book, and her expression was that of someone who definitely was not expecting to see her awkward-almost-one-night-stand in her living room less than twenty-four hours after the blessed event.

"Sorry. I meant to knock, but Jack let me in. Uh, but you look busy. I should go."

"No, I'm not busy. Sit down." She smiled at me then, and

maybe that weird expression had just been because she'd been expecting the person who walked into the room to be Jack. So, I sat down on the couch diagonal from her chair.

"Hi," I said again.

"Hi." She slid a bookmark into her book and tossed it on the coffee table.

"So . . . Óskar, like, told me you probably wouldn't want to hang out again. And that's fine. We can be friends or not friends or whatever. But I did"—I leaned closer and dropped my voice to a whisper, in case Óskar was lurking around the corner somewhere—"just want to say thanks for being so nice to me last night. Most people I know wouldn't have been so cool about it. I really appreciate that."

She smiled again, and it still seemed genuine. "You came all the way here to tell me that?"

"Yeah. Also, I want to use your kitchen."

"The kitchen?"

"Yeah. Can I make you dinner? It's not a romantic gesture. It's totally selfish. I just want, like, food that isn't from a restaurant or a plastic bag. And I can't cook at the hotel with just a microwave and teapot. Please, God, I just need twenty minutes with your stove."

She tilted her head back and laughed. "Yes, you can make dinner. What do you want to eat?"

After a lengthy debate about the pros and cons of my vegetarian diet, Björk and I searched the kitchen for something meatless. Eventually we unearthed a package of penne pasta and the stuff I needed to make "wodka" sauce. While waiting for the water to boil, I finally got up the nerve to ask where that beautiful blond bastard was hiding.

"Working."

"I thought he didn't work on the weekends."

"Not at the hotel. He is at his other job."

"What? I can't picture him at any other job. Except maybe, like, an air traffic controller or something. Ha!"

"He's interning at a studio. I'm surprised he hasn't mentioned it to you. He's very passionate about music."

Jack walked across the living room in front of us, still on the phone. He disappeared into Óskar's bedroom and came back wearing a jacket. Björk watched him walk out the front door and down the sidewalk.

"Thank God he is gone!" she said.

"I take it you're not a fan?" I asked, stirring the crushed tomatoes as they heated on the stove.

She gave me that don't-even-get-me-started look. "No one likes him. He's SHIT!" She raised a middle finger and waved it back and forth in the direction Jack had been heading. "He likes fucking little boys."

I asked if she meant that literally, and she said yes, that Jack had been with Óskar since he was twenty-seven and Óskar was fourteen.

"Holy hell!"

"See, that is the appropriate response," she said, gesturing to my disgusted face as she poured us both a glass of wine.

"Fourteen is legal here, but that doesn't mean Jack didn't take advantage of a child whose mother had just died and whose father was losing his mind. But you can't convince Óskar of that—"

"Óskar told me he wanted to break up with him."

"Did he? He says that every time Jack comes to visit, but he never will." She boosted herself up on the counter next to the stove and watched me stir the cream into the tomato sauce.

"Oh."

I guess I must have sounded pretty wounded, because Björk stared at me for a long while, then asked if I was gay. And I told her I wasn't much for labels—"queer, if you must" —and I thought I might be sort of into Óskar as of late. Then I apologized for last night. "You're beautiful and really amazing. But I'm a little confused."

"Only 'a little,' are you?" She reached over and raked her fingers through the side of my hair. "He talks about you all the time. If anyone can convince Óskar he doesn't need That Asshole Jack, it's you."

All I said was, "Huh," because my mind was too muddled to conjure something witty up. I didn't know how she could be so cool about everything, which made me feel relieved and anxious at the same time. I wanted her to keep telling me about Óskar. I had a million questions, but they burst like our glow-in-the-dark bubbles before I could even form the words. Then the timer went off and I had to drain the pasta.

He talks about me. All the time.

I have to say I made a pretty bitchin' pot of pasta, but I could barely eat. Björk asked me if I wanted to take the leftovers with me, but I said, "Nah. Óskar'll probably be hungry when he gets home, right?"

And she laughed, probably because I was being so weird and obvious, but she told me she'd make sure he got some.

"Could I ask you one more favor, please? You said you're studying to be a stylist. And—well, look at me. I could really use a haircut. Do you mind? I'll pay you, of course."

She wouldn't let me pay her—dinner was enough, she said. And I said, "But dinner was payment for the blowjob!" and she whacked me in the chest with the back of her hand. A few minutes later, I was sitting backwards in her kitchen chair with a sky-blue bath towel draped around my shoulders.

I must admit that damn towel had me harboring all sorts of absurd and inappropriate thoughts about a certain blue-eyed boy reaching for it as he emerged dripping wet from the bath. I've got it bad, V. For a tiny little Icelandic man. He's so scrawny-cute, though. Like a toy dog breed. A teacup Viking, if you will.

"Give me the 'Icelandic Male Under Forty,' please. Oh, don't look at me like that. You know damn good and well all the men here have the same haircut." They do. They totally do. All the guys under forty have that hipster haircut that is long on the top and buzzed short on the side. It's very European and chic.

The men over forty have THE WORST haircuts, by the way. They look like Javier Bardem in *No Country for Old Men*. Ugh.

Björk scoffed at me, but needed no further instructions. She grabbed her clippers and went to work. The haircut made me feel as bright and shiny as my new wardrobe. I gave Björk a quick goodbye hug and skipped on out of there.

And, now, just like that, I have this other thing. A mission. A new purpose. I want to convince Óskar to break up with Jack. I want to kiss him and wrap my arms around him, and, uhhh, more stuff than that.

Will it end badly? Yeah, probably. But I like the way I feel right now. And right now is all I have.

Miles Away to Vivian Girl

June 14 5:57 PM

Lazy Sunday. Today I've been anxious and jittery, full of energy. I *almost* went for a run, but, let's face it . . . that's just not going to happen. But I did go down to the spa and swim a few laps in the big pool, which gave me the illusion that I was getting in shape. I even faced the group showers, because it's Icelandic LAW that you get nude and scrub your bits before entering a public pool or hot spring. I actually managed to keep myself from jerking it this time. Haha.

I shaved. I ironed my good gray shirt. And then I figured I should probably Skype my mommies.

"Hello, darling. Did you get your hair cut? You look so grown up."

"Uh-huh. Looks like someone gave you a makeover as well."

Mamochka had on way too much blue eye shadow, and her hair was pulled to the side in a fishtail braid. "Yes, but they made me the wrong princess—"

"You should be Anastasia."

"Exactly!" She grinned, resting her chin on her hand as she looked into the camera. "But those kiddos wouldn't listen."

"I have to admit, I always kind of liked those impromptu makeover sessions the campers throw. I mean, let's face it, I look pretty damn good in eyeliner."

Mamochka threw her head back and laughed. Then we went on for a while, listing all the great costumes the campers had thrown together over the years. Jade's Bettie Page look and Johnny's perfect Vincent Price impersonations. And, of course, that time you dressed up like Jem from the Holograms. Somehow, the subject shifted to my art, and I told her about the miles.in.her.shoes Instagram and how I'd started photographing your boots.

"That's a wonderful idea."

"But that's it. An idea. It's just an abstract idea at this point. I think . . . I don't know. I want to do something, and I want it to be meaningful, but I'm having trouble grasping what the focus should be. All I can think of is posting these photos and maybe asking other people to submit. Like some sort of solidarity thing. I mean, if V were here, she'd know where to go with it."

"Well, what do you think she'd do if she were in YOUR shoes, Miles? What would she have done with the project?"

I stared past my iPad to the forest mural on the wall behind my bed. "She was always looking for kindred spirits. I think she'd use it to start a conversation with them."

"Yes. That does sound like her," Mamochka said. "So, what about you? Who do you need to start a conversation with?"

"Her followers, for one. I want them to know that she still really means a lot to me. She will always . . ." I sighed and sniffled a little bit.

"I think that's important. But who else?"

"I dunno."

"Maybe other people who've lost someone to suicide?"

"Yeah . . ."

"What are you thinking?"

"I guess I'm pretty pissed about the fact that we still live in a world where people are shamed and ridiculed for loving a transgender person. That sounds selfish, though. I don't want to make this about me."

"I don't think that's selfish at all, Miles. I think it's a very good conversation for you to begin."

So, after I got off the call, I logged into the new account Óskar had made for me, and I posted that first photo of your empty boots in the corner of my hotel room.

5 years ago, a beautiful transgender girl named Vivian came into my life.

3 years ago, we fell in love.

18 months ago, Vivian lapsed into a coma after an attempted suicide.

Today, I am trying to figure out how the hell to move forward now that my whole world seems gone. I'm an ocean away from her, my first solo trip. And I really need to know I'm not alone.

So, if you loved Vivian,

If you're trans or love someone who's trans,

Or if you know what it feels like to lose someone to suicide,

Snap a photo. Paint a picture. Write a poem. Do that thing you do better than anything else and share it. Seriously, guys, show me your shoes (especially if they're red—V's favorite color). #inhershoes

I need to know we're all still standing on solid ground.

It's been a few hours since I posted that, and I already have three replies. The first was a snapshot of two pairs of bare feet on a wooden boat dock. Both had red-painted toenails.

Sorry, Miles, but we're not wearing any shoes! xoxo, Mamochka and Mom.

The next was a drawing of a pair of red studded Mary Janes on a cracked sidewalk:

My boyfriend Max is the cutest transboy in the world. These used to be his!

And the last one, well . . . it's a blank, black video with a sound clip from someone called Converse_ly. There aren't any vocals, just an electric guitar and what sounds like a plinky toy piano. It's messy, but I think it's supposed to sound that way. First the guitar is too loud and fast, and the piano kind of slow, buried in the background. But as the music builds, the instruments kind of trade places, and at the end, the piano is the overpowering part. But for a moment, right in the middle, both parts play perfectly together.

There's no caption, and no other photos have been posted under the username. Hmm.

Miles Away to Vivian Girl
June 15 9:03 AM

I just woke up. The phone woke me up!

"Hello?"

"*Halló.*"

"Oscar? Shit. Sorry. I'm never going to remember to say your name right. But, it's you, isn't it?"

"Mmm-hmm."

"Hi." GOD MILES SHUT UP!

"You have some mail. Would you like me to bring it up?"

"Uh, no. I'll be down for breakfast in a few minutes."

Yes! He's here! Of course, this probably means that he hasn't ditched Jack yet. But it also means that I get to go see him. Right now.

Miles Away to Vivian Girl

June 15 10:14 AM

Well. I got my debit card. That's good, right? I also got a package from Mamochka, which I opened at breakfast. There's a mushy little note and a T-shirt from Camp. Some candy. The front of the T-shirt says HAPPY CAMPER, and it has a little stylized campfire emblem.

Another ironic T-shirt for Miles. Yay.

Because right now I am NOT a Happy Camper. I'm an Idiotic Camper. A Homesick Camper. A Delusional Camper.

On the elevator ride, I pictured myself walking into the lobby, and I'd see Óskar and, like, fucking . . . I dunno . . . "It's Oh So Quiet" would play on the soundtrack to my life. He'd be Weekend Óskar with disheveled hair and bad boy clothes, but ACTUALLY I get down there, and it's Óskar with his hair up and That Asshole Jack with his arm around Óskar's chair. I look at them and they're both so perfect and fashionably European and I could never . . . I mean, why bother?

Fuck. I'm such an idiot. Fuck.

chapter sixteen

Miles Away to Vivian Girl

June 15 10:03 PM

The thing about crushes, though, is that just when you've written them off—too much trouble, a disaster waiting to happen—they show up all cute at your door, five thirty in the Icelandic afternoon. Don't you hate when that happens?

"Have you been to the penis museum?" he asked as he stepped past me into the room and plopped down on the corner of my unmade bed. He had a toolbox, one of those little red metal ones that everyone and their mom has.

"Are you coming on to me?" I stood in the doorway with my arms across my chest. Still a little mad at him for . . . being unavailable, I guess?

He turned his face and laughed with his hand over his mouth. Trying to hide that goofy-ass grin of his, probably.

Óskar laughing on my bed was probably the sexiest thing I've seen in a while.

"What's with the toolbox?"

"I told Yak I was fixing your shower. I hate when he comes to work. Been trying to escape him all day. You didn't take the hint when I offered to bring your mail this morning."

"Oh, sorry."

"You have plans right now? Let's escape." He rubbed his fingertips along his jawline, looking all thoughtful and mischievous. Cute.

So we snuck out a side door and booked it to the bus stop, Óskar's toolbox clanging as he ran. He sat close to me on the bus, with his knee pressed against mine. I stared at it most of the trip to Laugavegur, thinking, *I am NOT imagining this.*

So, the penis museum (or the Icelandic Phallological Museum, as it is properly called) is . . . just like it sounds. Just . . . blehhh. Jars and jars of formaldehyde-pickled dicks from all the animals in the kingdom. Oh, and some are mounted on the wall, like prize fish.

"I don't know why you brought me here," I said. "As a male and a vegetarian, I am deeply, deeply appalled."

"Look. Sperm whale. The biggest one." Óskar ran his fingers down a massive glass tube with this huge blubbery . . . BLEHHH!

"Ghhhhuh." I shuddered.

"Now I'm hungry for hot dogs." And after we left the museum, we did, in fact stroll down the street to the hot dog stand, where Óskar bought two dogs and a Coke. There's a little wooden picnic table next to the stand, with slats built in the top for holding your spare hot dog while you wolf down the first.

"Literally the best food in Iceland," Óskar said. "You should try it. I won't tell anyone."

"Nah, I'm good." Actually, I was starving.

"It's already dead and paid for. If you don't eat it, then I will, so there's no loss. Know what I mean?"

"Yeah . . . but I'm still not eating that."

He finished the first one and reached for the second. "I should joke about how you refused my wiener."

"You really are a dirty old man." I was blushing again. That's saying something, right? There's enough sexual tension between us that he could get me, the perpetual potty mouth, all bothered by a dick joke.

"Charming, isn't it?" He got up from the table and tossed his wrappers. "Where now? Where haven't you been?"

I thought about his mysterious other job that Björk had told me about. I raised my eyebrows and said, "I haven't been to . . . uh . . . a recording studio."

"Ah, I know where we should go next." Then he bolted down the street. Like, full-on ran. It was seven thirty on a Monday, so there weren't a ton of people out and about. I chased after him, trying my best to keep up, but when the gap between us grew to two blocks, he finally slowed down and let me catch up. He teased me about being out of shape, and I wheezed out something about how I used to be a fat kid.

The next stop on Óskar's Impromptu Tour of Reykjavik was 12 Tónar. It's a little green and white house-like building with two big picture windows on the front. I've been meaning to go there, as I've read it's one of the best record stores in the world. Like Iceland itself, it's a little underwhelming upon your arrival. It's tiny and rundown, nothing too impressive. The guy at the counter seemed to know Óskar, but I've read that everyone in Iceland knows one another. Only three hundred thousand people. They have an app that lets them check and make sure their Friday night hookup isn't related to them, because I guess that's a problem. While Óskar and the shop guy chatted, I browsed around trying to decipher their Icelandic. Nope, nothing. The guy made Óskar a cup of coffee and asked if I wanted some, but I declined.

"He doesn't like it," Óskar explained. Coffee in one hand, stack of CDs in the other, he led me down a rickety spiral staircase to a little basement room. There were more CDs in displays and cardboard boxes everywhere and some old-fashioned furniture. We sat side by side on a blue velvet couch with carved wooden trim. Knees touching again . . .

I smiled to myself about that. And about how Óskar remembered me saying I don't like coffee. That's such a small, random detail.

I picked at a loose thread on my jeans while Óskar sorted through the CDs in his lap. The cool thing about 12 Tónar, the reason everyone says it's the best, is because you can literally listen to any CD you want—open it up, fondle the liner notes, stare at your reflection in the silvery rainbow disc. On the coffee table in front of the couch, there were a couple of little boom boxes. Óskar popped in a disc and passed me the headphones. It was a trashy pop song, a girl singing about dance floors and booty shorts.

"This is awful," I said, probably too loudly because of the headphones.

He unrolled the album booklet and pointed to a line of text—*lyrics by Óskar Franz Magnússon.*

"What, no! That's you? You wrote these atrocious lyrics?" I cackled. "And your middle name is Franz?"

He pulled the headphones away, and his mouth was close to my ear. "I whore myself out. Here, let me play you something better."

We moved through a stack of discs—fast guitar rhythms that were so mathematically perfect they made my head spin, bluesy R & B, oddly cheerful Icelandic hip-hop, dark heavy metal, and folksy rock with swooning vocals. Óskar's name was on all of it somewhere—lyrics, guitars, synths, even violin.

"Dude, you are super talented. I'm always so jealous of people who can do music. I couldn't even play my recorder."

"What's a recorder?"

"Oh, this little plastic instrument that American elementary school kids are forced to learn. So how'd you get on all these albums?"

"The studio hires me when they need extra musicians. It's my backup job."

"THIS is your backup job?"

He shrugged and checked his watch and he rose from the sofa. "One more stop, and then maybe I'll let you see me play."

The next place he took me was Harpa, the concert hall.

"Goddamn, I wish I had my camera." Like the airport, this place was all glass and light and angles. It was like being inside a Christmas ornament. Or, no, a kaleidoscope.

"What about your mobile?"

"Screen's busted. Guess I'll have to come back."

"Orrr, just look. Keep it in here." He pointed to his chest.

"Right. Damn the megapixels." I looked at him, and he looked past me, like he always does.

We walked along the high side wall that's constructed from thousands of elongated hexagons of glass. There were lots of tourists around us, snapping pictures and chasing their children in circles. But the place was so big, the ceiling so tall, that there was space enough for us to feel alone together. Me and Óskar. And my heart was kind of convulsing from all the information I was trying to pack in—but mainly because I wanted to kiss him. I sooo wanted to kiss him.

I like Óskar so much because when he's around, I stop thinking of you. Or, if I do, it's distant and fuzzy, like I really am doing what Mom said I should. Like, I really am learning to let you go.

When we got to the corner, I wrapped my arm around his waist and pulled him in. I put a finger under his chin and tilted his face toward me. Close enough that we could kiss, but I let him be the one to choose whether or not he wanted to bridge that tiny gap between my mouth and his.

My heart was drumming out Óskaresque mathematical rhythms, and maybe I was hearing his beats mingled with mine. My fingertips digging into his tightly wound hair.

We stayed like that for three eternal seconds. I bet we looked like weirdoes to the tourists. Or maybe they were disgusted by the two men almost kissing. Or maybe someone saw us silhouetted by multicolored glass and light and thought we looked like a painting, so they snapped a picture and now this almost-kiss will forever be in their Icelandic memories.

Then Óskar took a step back. And I took a step back. He smoothed his shirt, even though it was flawless, and raised a hand like I was a threat he needed to subdue.

"I have a boyfriend."

"Yeah, I know."

We retraced our steps out of the building, and back on the street, Óskar said, "The funny thing is that Yak isn't normally around. He lives in Wales. I see him only a few times a year. He doesn't mind if I sleep with other men. I do sometimes, and I'm sure he has other lovers than me. But the rule is that when we're together, we're together. Nobody else."

"Yeah. Okay. Sorry."

"You don't have to be sorry. I want to—the first weekend you were here, I thought I'd take you on the *rúntur* and maybe we'd hook up. But you already had plans."

My night with Shannon. I couldn't believe Óskar'd been into me for that long. "Well, shit."

He shrugged. "And then Yak showed up unannounced. I don't know what to do with him. I adore him when he isn't next to me. But when he is, I feel so trapped."

"When's he leaving again?"

"I don't know."

Hands in our pockets, we ended up wandering the road that winds along the seashore. I probably should have just dunked my head in. God. We passed that sculpture that looks like the skeletal remains of a Viking boat. It surprised me that Óskar didn't stop. I think maybe he'd just phased out of impress-the-tourist mode. He probably walks past those ship bones every day. Nothing new.

So, I didn't stop either, or point them out. I just kept walking next to him, pretending for a moment that I could be a part of Óskar's everyday life.

"I'm learning to be a producer," he said as we approached a long pale yellow building with LAZY LUNA RECORDING STUDIO on the sign. A crooked crescent moon hung on the door. "That's my dream. I'm a behind-the-scenes kind of guy." He winked at me.

I was exhausted. From the long walk, but also just emotionally. I needed that fluffy white hotel bed. And I missed home. I missed my everyday life. I wouldn't be any better or worse off in either place, but at least the food was better at home. I'd have comfortable shitty clothes and video games and Mamochka if I were home.

And darkness. I miss darkness. Fireflies.

The owner of the recording studio, a beardly guy named Siggi, handed Óskar a pile of sheet music and the two of them sifted through it while I stared at the gangster movie playing on the TV in Siggi's office. Finally Óskar chose a few pieces he wanted to work on, and we moved from the office to the studio. It looked like you'd imagine—a room with a big mixing board facing another room lined with soundproof glass. Óskar went into the recording booth while Siggi and I sat in chairs by the soundboard.

"Cheer up," Óskar said to me through the glass. We could hear him, but he couldn't hear us unless Siggi pressed a button. "There's some Brennivín in my toolbox."

"I don't even know what that is."

"Black Death," Siggi said, because Óskar didn't know I'd replied.

The toolbox was on the floor under the soundboard. I popped it open. There was a single socket wrench, a Phillips-head screwdriver, a mini tape measure, and a big green bottle of alcohol. Oh, also there was an iPhone. I didn't even know Óskar had an iPhone.

Yep, everything he needed to fix my imaginary shower problems, right?

I unscrewed the cap and found out from just one whiff

why they call that shit Black Death. "Maybe later," I said, and Siggi laughed at me. I offered him the bottle, but apparently it's all fine and dandy in Iceland if you wanna binge your brains out on Friday and Saturday, but if you glance at so much as a beer the rest of the week, you're a raging alcoholic.

Behind the glass, Óskar started to undress. And I started to wonder if I needed that booze after all. First he undid his bowtie, then he unbuttoned and shrugged off his work shirt. He had a light pink shirt on underneath, and he tugged that over his head, too. The pants stayed on (thankfully), but I could see the waistband of his lavender briefs peeking out. Lastly, he peeled off his shoes and socks.

"Watch this," Siggi said. "Sexy librarian in three . . . two . . . one."

And, though he wasn't paying a bit of attention to either of us, Óskar pulled the elastic band from his bun and shook out his hair, right on cue.

I melted into my chair. And I stayed in that liquid state pretty much the entire time Óskar was playing. At one point, Siggi looked over at me and asked if I was Jack.

"Fuck no. I'm Miles."

Anyway, I sat there all starry-eyed, watching Óskar work his way through the sheet music. Sometimes he would break out a pencil and scribble on the pages, humming out a different set of notes that he and Siggi would argue over. Eventually, they'd come to an agreement, and Óskar would pick up a guitar or a pair of drumsticks or whatever, and Siggi would record him playing. It always sounded perfect to me, but one or the other of them would want a third or fourth or fifth take. And as much as I liked watching Óskar play, I eventually nodded off. When I woke up, Siggi had gone out for a ciggy and Óskar was hunched over some more sheet music. The iPhone was ringing inside his toolbox. I dug it out.

Jack, of course.

I couldn't find the button to press to talk to Óskar, but he saw me moving and came up to the glass. I held the phone up so he could see Jack was calling.

"Shit. I forgot to change phones. Turn it off for me. Immediately. Thanks." Later he told me that Jack uses one of those family tracker apps to keep tabs on him, and normally when he wants to go somewhere without Jack knowing, he swaps his SIM into the old flip phone and leaves his iPhone at the hotel.

"We should go. I don't want him coming here."

I looked for the button again but still couldn't find it in the sea of sliders and knobs. Óskar was pressed against the glass, with his hands near his face. I gave up on finding the button and just looked up at him. I traced my hand down the soundproof glass, over his chest and down to his fucking six-pack, and I swear I could almost feel the heat of him. I thought about the magic words Björk had told me to say. I looked up at his blinky blue eyes and hoped he could read lips.

"You don't need him."

But I'm not really sure if I was saying it to Óskar or myself.

We took a bus back to the main hub, and then it was time to part ways. He could have left right then and walked the block or two back home, but he waited with me for the next bus back to the hotel to arrive.

"I know it's none of my business, but have you really been with him since you were fourteen?"

He nodded.

"And how old are you now?"

"Twenty."

"Six years. That's a long time."

"Yes. A wery long time." He balanced himself on the curb, with the scuffed toes of his Chucks dangling over the street.

"We're kind of in the same place, you know? Just suffering through this relationship that doesn't fit us anymore. You said ending things with him would be complicated, but, man, you should try breaking up with someone in a coma."

"Everyone hates Yak. They all wanted me to go to therapy—Karl, Bryndis, Björk. So, I did. They believed that after some time, I'd have a revelation and see him differently. But after all these years, I don't have any regrets. He was kind and patient. He didn't abuse me. He didn't even pressure me—I gave myself to him when I was ready. I never felt like a victim. He took care of me when I really needed someone to take care of me. I don't think my opinion on those matters will ever change."

"I'm sensing a *but* . . ."

"Yes, but . . . I don't need him taking care of me anymore. And . . . I worry that my friends are right. When I remove myself from the equation and picture just . . . some boy off the street in little Óskar's shoes, I do understand the concern. My opinions may never change, but that doesn't mean that they aren't wrong."

I stared at him. "You're really fucking smart, you know that?"

"You're smart, too. You sometimes say such intelligent things, but then you downplay them with *fucks* and *likes* and *whatevers*."

"Maybe. Hey, you know what? I'm kinda glad we didn't hang out or hook up or anything on that first weekend. 'Cause you probably would have been all Icelandic about it and never spoken to me again. And I like talking to you. Tell me something else."

"That's it, really. The seed has been planted, and I keep watering it with the idea that perhaps there have been other little Óskars, you know? And sometimes I think I stay with Yak because I feel it is my burden to protect these faceless little boys. I often wonder what he's gotten up to while he's been away. And what he'll do if I'm gone from him for good. There is this one question my therapist asks that I've been unable to answer: have my friends' opinions poisoned Yak for me, or could he actually be poison? I don't know. But that means I don't trust him. And if I don't trust him, does he belong in my life?"

It seemed like a rhetorical question, so I let it hang in the air for a moment, then I leaned in. "So, Óskar"—and, yes, I said his name correctly that time—"what is Wednesday?"

"The seventeenth."

"What else?"

"Icelandic National Day."

"Also known as . . . ?"

"Our independence day."

"Exactly. Yeah." The bus was coming, and I stepped up to the curb. "OUR independence day. I'm going to rent a car and get the fuck outta Reykjavik for a week. You should ditch Jack and join me, man. Think about it."

Then I got on the bus without waiting for an answer. Without looking back.

chapter seventeen

Miles Away to Vivian Girl

June 16 3:34 PM

I think I'm ready for my road trip. I spent the morning at the hotel desk with Óskar and Atli, with That Asshole Jack peering over their shoulders. They helped me rent a car and some camping equipment. Also, getting my phone screen fixed was on the list for today. I wasn't going to bother, but since I'm going to be out in BFE, I decided it'd be a good idea. I was like, "Do you know a guy who fixes phones?" Because, you know, everyone knows a guy. And it turns out Atli is that guy. He's fixing it after work and will bring it back later this evening. And he didn't charge me an arm and a leg, so that's cool.

Speaking of saving money, Óskar and Atli spent like an hour trying to convince me that I should hitchhike. Apparently it's safe here, totally the norm. But I'm wary. And I think I also need the control. I want to be able to go where I want, when I want, and not be an inconvenience to someone who's just trying to be nice. But, anyway, the rental car seems pretty cool. Comes with a GPS that's preprogrammed to guide me to all the interesting places on the Ring Road, the main roadway that loops around the island. The rental company dropped it off at the hotel, and I've already driven it once. I went downtown to pick up the camping supplies I'd rented: tent, cooler, cookware, etc. The other thing I bought in town was this camper's card that gives me access to practically every campsite in Iceland.

Also, earlier, Óskar, Atli, and I had a lengthy argument about "hiring" versus "renting," because every time I'd say "rent," Óskar'd say "hire," and I was like, "Look, little man, you cannot hire an inanimate object."

Jack mostly stayed in the background and scowled.

"How many sleeping bags did I rent?"

"You hired two."

"Are they coming to trim the rosebushes and clean my gutters?"

Anyway . . . I didn't pick the number of sleeping bags. Óskar did, so . . . I decided to take that as a positive sign. But I couldn't exactly ask with That Asshole Jack looming around.

I went grocery shopping, too. Enough to feed two or three with each meal. Even if Óskar flakes, it never hurts to have extra food on a campground. That's how you make friends.

I bought another box of condoms.

And a few minutes ago, I called down to the front desk to tell Óskar I'm leaving bright and early tomorrow. Seven a.m.

Miles Away to Vivian Girl

I'm fidgety again. And I think I'm idiotic. I should hope and pray that Óskar doesn't show up tomorrow. I can sit here and tell myself that I'm helping Óskar by conning him into ditching Jack, but getting involved with me is probably worse than staying where he's at.

No, I'm not worse than that asshole. But I'm no prize either.

In other news, it is nice to have my phone back again. Phone photography is an art in and of itself. I've already been experimenting with some apps and filters and stuff. There is a magic to it that I think most people aren't willing to admit. That beauty can come from something so soul-sucking. Sure, I might get lost on Twitter, or I might make something cool. Whatever helps, helps.

I spent some time earlier wondering if you'd like Óskar. At first I thought no, you wouldn't. And I felt a little guilty about that, the fact that the first person I've been genuinely interested in after you is someone you wouldn't approve of. But then I thought maybe you would if you just gave him some time.

You'd like Óskar's accent, for starters, and you'd make him pronounce things for you. And I wonder if he'd like you, if he'd sound his way through *hamburger* and *alligator* for you, simply because you are always the most sparkling person in the room.

And I bet you could make him laugh, if you figured out how to hold his interest long enough. Of course, I'd be more entertained by this conversation than anyone. And happy about it, too. Because it's a fantasy. It belongs in a future none of us will ever have.

Miles Away to Vivian Girl

June 16 9:15 PM

Since I've been feeling pretty down on myself, I decided to check the Instagram account. I had 13 followers the other day, and now I have 176, wow! And there are 59 photos with the inhershoes hashtag. I've been trying to talk to all of them, leave comments, you know? I'm not great at talking to strangers, especially about something big and important like this. It makes me happy, though, to think I started something. To watch that ripple effect.

Miles Away to Vivian Girl

June 16 11:19 PM

Óskar showed up an hour ago. He stood in the doorway, and we just kind of looked at each other for a second. I think we were deciding if we were going to make out. Then he walked past me and plopped down on the corner of my bed like he did the other day, only he wasn't laughing this time.

He said he couldn't go with me tomorrow. And I said okay. He sat there for a second and then he said he wanted to, but it would cause too much trouble. And I said, "I know."

And he said, "You don't know everything," but not, like, in a snarky way. He just meant I didn't know all the details. Then he went on to tell me all the details.

So, like a year ago when Óskar got your painting, he ended up on Mamochka and Mom's email list, and occasionally he'd receive those letters they send out, updating everyone about you. Everyone who donates gets the letters, but Óskar decided to email back.

I asked why, and he said, "Because I promised everyone I'd see a therapist."

OMFG, Óskar is one of Mom's patients. He said he sees her via Skype. I knew there was something going on. All this time I thought maybe Mamochka was behind this, but it was Mom. I can't believe this shit. How did I not realize?

I was like, "Wait. I do her billing. I've never mailed anything to Iceland. And a name like Óskar Franz Magnússon is kinda hard to forget—"

"Jack monitors my finances, and I didn't want him to know. So she and I bartered." He pointed to the floor. "This is my therapy bill. As the manager of this hotel, I'm able to provide you with a free stay. But if I leave Jack, I leave the job. And I'm certain that will mean you must leave the hotel."

"So, what?" I said. "I'm going to be gone camping for a week. And then I only have another week after that. I'll find another hotel."

"It's tourist season. I've been calling around, but many places are booked."

"Then I'll camp for two weeks if I have to, all right?" I sat next to him on the bed. Knees touching. "Look, if you think it's time to break up with him, then just break up with him, okay? Don't make this about me."

"I don't even know where I'll live after . . . if I . . ." He sighed. "How did you get so far?"

"Uh, I took a plane?"

"Why do you do that? You know what I mean! You're . . ." He wove his fingers together in his lap. "Brave. You're just as intelligent and brave as your mother said you were. I've been anxious to meet you for some time."

My fucking parents . . . Just like how when Mamochka found out you had a crush on me, she harassed me a million times to give you a chance. Mom has shipped me off to Viking Wonder Boy, knowing damn good and well I'd go all head over heels for him, too.

I'm going to have to have a little chat with them once I finish messaging you.

"Oh, man. That's adorable that you think I'm brave and shit. And smart. Fucking hilarious. I'm a moron. And I'm in pain, like, all the time. I'm terrified of everything, like . . . damn buses."

He scoffed at me, and I scoffed at him.

I wanted to kiss him. Just a little kiss, right below his ear.

"It's a rare trait, though, to be able to see when something is wrong and to know when to walk away. I admire that."

"Oh, shut up. You're embarrassing me."

He leaned in. "Also, did you know that you're really fucking sexy?"

"God." I buried my face in my hands. "You'resexytoo."

"I should go. I have a very long letter to write. Bags to pack. That sort of thing." I felt the bed rise as he hopped up. "I'll see you tomorrow."

"Promise me," I growled. "Promise me I'm not going to lay here all night thinking about you and then have you fucking blow me off."

"I promise to do some of those verbs with you in the near future."

Lay. Fucking. Blow . . . Right. "Dirty old man." I grinned into my hands.

Miles Away to Vivian Girl

June 17 9:45 PM

I didn't know when I'd get to message you again, but this campground has Wi-Fi, so here I am. It's been an incredibly long day. Óskar's out cold (archangel status: 100 percent), and I'm close to drifting myself.

Mom once told me that the ultimate test of any relationship was furniture assembly. That always kind of scared the shit out of me, so I paid extra to have that bookshelf we got for your cabin put together at the store. I didn't want cheap particle-board furniture to spell our demise.

But, anyway, tent assembly is probably just as frustrating, and I'm happy to say that Mr. Magnússon and I passed with flying colors. We work together perfectly, as a matter of fact. I kind of dove in, matching pieces as I saw fit, and he was the one who stopped to read the directions, coming behind me to correct my mistakes and add some stability. We didn't fight; we didn't even talk, really. We didn't need to. We just . . . clicked.

The rest of the day was different, though. Óskar showed up while I was loading the car. Weekend Óskar with messy hair and blue jeans. I could tell he hadn't slept. He really did write Jack a big, long Dear John letter. I didn't read it or anything, but I saw him stuff it in a manila envelope with his iPhone and a set of keys. Then he went into the hotel and put it on the desk in his old office. He came back to the car with two cups of coffee and then remembered I don't like coffee and immediately apologized.

"I can get you some tea."

"No big deal. Forget that, dude. You're not a concierge anymore, okay? You ready to do this?"

He sighed and tossed his backpack into the trunk. "Let's go."

So, the first thing that I really wanted to knock out of the way was the Golden Circle. It's the little route that takes you through some of the more popular landmarks—the first being Thingvellir National Park. So I turned on the GPS and hit the highway. About ten, fifteen minutes into our trip, I looked over and saw that Óskar was crying.

Well, shit.

That's when I realized what an asshole I really am. I had

it in my head that this trip would be all hot springs and hand jobs. I hadn't even considered the fact that I'd just badgered a practical stranger into ending a long-term relationship for a two-week road trip. Óskar is going to need to grieve. Even if things were shitty, six years is a long time. You don't just end a relationship like that and go off fucking some dude from Missouri. Well, okay, some people would. But not Óskar.

I opened my mouth, and he immediately cut me off. "Don't try to talk to me now."

I know I don't know him very well, but I can tell he hates crying. So, I pulled my auxiliary cable out of the console and plugged in my phone. "Wanna hear some Smiths, ya sad bastard?"

He smiled a little. "Anything but 'This Charming Man.'"

"We'll skip that one," I said. "'Girlfriend in a Coma' too."

So, we drove straight through *Louder Than Bombs* until we got to the park. There were a few places I might have stopped along the way to photograph, but I felt like we needed to put some distance between us and Reykjavik. I didn't want to be within reach when Jack finally woke up and found that letter.

When I could see we were getting close to the park, I turned the music down and asked Óskar if he'd been there before. He said he had and that as soon as we got there, we should make a cairn. He wasn't crying anymore.

I said I didn't know what a cairn was, but I'd be down for making whatever.

The first thing you see when you get to Thingvellir is this giant field with thousands of neatly piled stacks of rocks—the cairns. Now that I know what they are, I realize I've seen them everywhere. Even that first day, traveling from Keflavik to Reykjavik, I remember seeing these piles of stones all along the highway.

"So . . . are they, like, fairy houses or something?" I asked as we approached the field of cairns.

He just looked at me like I was a moron. "They're path markers from back before Iceland had roads."

"Whoa."

"Of course, nobody is marking a pathway here. This is just for fun," he said, gesturing in front of us, where all across the field people were constructing their own little piles of rocks.

"I would like to respectfully disagree, man. Everyone here is marking their own path."

He nodded. "True."

So, we went and gathered our stones and then chose a spot in the field. Óskar isn't afraid to get his hands dirty, and he appears to be able to carry ten times his weight in rocks, like some sort of human/ant hybrid.

It sounds kind of stupid, but building this little pyramid of rocks with him was really soothing. Like our quiet mornings together at the breakfast buffet, I found myself caught up in Óskar's personal bubble of calm. I tried not to overthink, just let him lead the way. I figured we were just going to stack some shit together and leave—like, how could we possibly make our stack of rocks look different from a thousand other stacks of rocks?

But I forgot I was traveling with an expert-level Jenga player. Our cairn did look like all the others—until Óskar worked his magic. He circled the cairn, carefully pulling out stones here and there. And by the time he was done, it wasn't a messy pile, but this intricate swirling thing. It was mathematical, intense. Like his guitar solos. Or a DNA strand.

It was beautiful.

And before I could even photograph it, some bratty little kids stormed through and knocked it over. I screamed at them for being shitheads, but I don't think they understood English.

"Sorry, Óskar."

"Not a problem. It wasn't meant to last."

And then we hiked around the park for a little bit. The cool thing is that there's this big blue-green lake and you can also see where the continental plates have shifted, leaving a huge gap. That was actually the only time I stopped to photograph your boots today.

We stopped for lunch at a picnic area, and I made us some quesadillas, which Óskar seemed to really enjoy. I asked him how he liked the pasta I made the other night, and he frowned and told me Jack ate it all before he got home from work. That asshole.

While we were there, I made use of the free Wi-Fi and uploaded that picture of your boots next to the continental drift.

Allow me, for a moment, I wrote, to take us back to third grade science class. This is the Mid-Atlantic Ridge, the place where the North American and Eurasian tectonic plates are slowly, slowly tearing apart. It sounds so destructive, doesn't it? Like the world could just keep spreading and eventually it'll just crack in half and bleed out into the universe. But the good news is that it doesn't actually work like that. When the earth splits, lava rises and cools, creating new land where there wasn't any before. It heals as it tears. I think humans do that, too. So, anyway, this is the tenth photo I've taken of Vivian's boots, and it might be my last for a little while. I do want to keep connecting and keep exploring this new scar tissue. You might be seeing some pics of my camping trip soon, or maybe some radio silence for a while. But know that I'll be around and scoping out the hashtag when I can. Sincerely, your favorite molten rock lava boy, Miles.

Next we drove to Geysir, the geyser for which all others are named. It's inactive now, but there's another one nearby called Strokkur that goes off every ten minutes or so. I snapped a few photos and tried to convince Óskar to lie down and let me frame a picture making it look like the geyser was shooting out of his mouth—but he was not down for that shit.

"Are you ever going to let me take a picture of you?" I asked. Other than the one I snuck of him walking away from me on our beer run, I don't have a single photo of Óskar.

— 224 —

"I'm not scenery," he said. "Not some pretty landscape for you to sell or show off to your friends."

The tone of his voice surprised me. He'd never snapped at me like that. I put the lens cap back on my camera and walked toward him. Behind him, the geyser went off, speckling both of us with mist.

"Sorry." He put his hand up, and at first he seemed to be blocking me from giving him a hug. But his fingertips grazed my shoulder and he leaned into me. "That should not have been directed at you."

I just grabbed him and told him it was all right, but really I was thinking of places to dump a body. Fucking Jack, man.

The third thing on the Golden Circle is Gullfoss, which I liked the best. It's these enormous falls. You can get really close, and the spray settles down over you, casting rainbows all over the place. Óskar told me that, in the nineteenth century, Gullfoss was set to be turned into a power plant, but this lady walked, like, seventy miles and threatened to throw herself over the edge in protest. And she won—they canceled the plans for the power plant.

I like stories like that.

It seemed like we'd done enough sightseeing for the day. We drove to the nearest campground and started setting up. I guess tomorrow we're going to drive along the south coast. I already saw some of it when I went on that tour, but I'm looking forward to letting Óskar show me around.

I'm also looking forward to sleeping next to him.

chapter eighteen

Miles Away to Vivian Girl

June 19 5:54 PM

Yesterday morning when I woke up, rain was beating down on the tent, dripping down the wall on Óskar's side. And he was gone. I groaned to myself, feeling so stupid and lonely again. Then I saw his backpack, and all that fear and paranoia slithered back up my spine to wherever it normally hides.

Óskar showed up a few minutes later, shaking droplets off the hood of his raincoat. *"Gódan daginn."*

I smiled because he'd never spoken to me in Icelandic before. "Hey."

He'd gone to the campground showers to get cleaned up and change, so I headed out to do the same. When I got back, he'd already disassembled the tent and loaded it up in the car. I could see that blond head of his bobbing in the driver's seat, giant headphones strapped to his ears. I slid into the passenger side and thanked him for packing up.

"No problem. I have a raincoat, and you don't."

"I wouldn't have melted," I said.

"Can I drive today?"

"Yeah. Sure." I started chewing on the ends of that paracord bracelet you made me two years ago at Camp. The one with the little sloth bead. You said it was my merit badge for being the laziest counselor at Camp. And then I threw my dream catcher like a Frisbee and accidentally hit Jade in the temple. And thus began the Great Craft War of '13. Those were the days.

Óskar was eating these peanut butter sandwich cookies I'd bought. He offered me the open package, and I scooped a few up. We sat there in silence for a bit, just stuffing our faces with junk food and watching the rain pelt down. The blurry, marbled windows gave me that same alone-in-public feeling as the day we'd almost kissed in the concert hall. But none of those romantic feels were there this time, just melancholy. I wasn't sure I'd ever get that kiss I'd been wanting.

When he was done eating, Óskar pulled his headphones down and started the car.

I reached for the stereo knob, turning the radio down to a murmur so I could talk to him. "How are you feeling today?"

"Internally directionless." Eeenternalleh Di-Rrrection-leees.

"Story of my life."

"Outwardly, though," he continued, "I have a plan. I was

thinking that—if you do not mind—that since it is raining, maybe we could visit my family today? I need to speak with Karl."

"Yeah, of course."

"I'm sorry—always involving you in such personal things. It's awkward."

"Oh, like I don't do the same thing to you!" I laughed. "It's easier sometimes, isn't it? To go through shit with someone you don't really know? I mean, it's like . . . the people who supposedly know you sort of unconsciously put all these expectations on you, and you find yourself behaving in accordance with that. But, like, in the presence of a stranger, you set your own expectations, you know? You become a truer version of yourself, maybe? Or at least get a little bit closer to the person you subconsciously want to be."

He blinked at me a couple times, then went back to watching the road. His mouth curved up just the tiniest bit.

"Sorry," I mumbled. "I'm rambling."

"I like it. I like the way you don't sanitize your words for me." He told me that people staying at the hotel tended to try to dumb stuff down for him, assuming he couldn't understand English well. I'd never even thought of that before—how he must have to concentrate to decode my babble from English to Icelandic, and vice versa for his replies. All that blinking he does is probably from moments lost in translation. He's been doing all the work in these conversations of ours. I wondered what it'd have been like if we'd been born into the same native language.

I found myself getting a little antsy when we passed the turnoff for that pool where I got some sense knocked into me. It already seemed like a million years ago; the bruise on my face is just a slightly darkened smudge.

"Can we try something?" I asked, and without waiting for his reply, I plucked his hand off the steering wheel and wove my fingers through his.

Óskar scowled at me. But he definitely didn't let go.

The thing I keep hearing about Icelanders and dating is basically that they don't do it. Supposedly they just get drunk and screw around on Friday nights, and if, perhaps, you find yourself in the same person's bed a few weekends in a row, the two of you might start to hang out together during sober daylight hours. And if that goes okay, then maybe you end up as a couple. There's a carefree casualness about it, but, personally, I'm a fucking sucker for a smidge of romance.

And since Óskar's spent the past six years being pampered by Handsome McBritishPants, then I figured he might like that sort of thing, too.

Sexual tension is, like, the best/worst thing in existence, right? I rubbed my thumb across his palm and examined his fingertips. "Yep, these are some nice phalanges. Excellently shaped metacarpals, might I add?"

Then he smiled his dorky smile, and we drove the rest

of the way to his family's house with our hands resting in my lap.

"Would you mind going to the door and asking Karl to meet me in the barn? Normally I call, but I abandoned my phone."

"Uh, sure." I disentangled my hand and dashed up to the house in the rain.

Óskar's dad answered the door. It's hard to believe that crumpled old man spawned the Icelandic Ken doll I'd left in the car. Their eyes are the same, though, and Óskar's dad is equally petite.

Like me, he was still a little bruised-up around the eyes.

He said something to me in Icelandic, and I said, "I don't speak Icelandic," and then he said something else in Icelandic.

"Karl," I said. "I'm looking for Karl." I said *Karl* American-style.

"Khaaruhl?" All right, so now we know where Óskar gets his pronunciation pickiness from.

I waited in the entryway while Óskar's dad went to get his eldest son.

"Hi, uh. I'm supposed to pass along the message that your brother is waiting in the barn," I told Karl when he showed up and said hello. I don't think he remembered me from the five minutes he'd seen me last week.

"Brother?" I heard their dad say in the background. Or probably he said it in Icelandic—*bróðir*. "Óskar?"

"Tell him to come in the house," Karl whispered. "Pabbi"

—another word I had to Google (Dad)—"has been asking for him."

"Are you sure it's safe?" I asked.

And then Karl got this look on his face like he realized who I was. "It is safe. He isn't like that all the time."

So I went all the way to the barn and told Óskar his dad was having a good day, and Óskar goes, "But I need to speak to Karl alone." So then I had to go back to the house (at least Óskar gave me his raincoat that time) and ask Karl again to go to the barn. It felt like playground gossiping.

So, anyway, Karl finally went to the barn, and I *think* Óskar told him that he broke up with Jack (I definitely heard a *Yak* in there), and Karl just grabbed him and hugged him for the longest time. I left them to talk, and wandered toward the other end of the barn where some sheep were chilling in their stalls. Some of them were friendly and let me pet them, but others skittered away.

"Do you eat them?" I asked when Óskar showed up and leaned against one of the gates. Karl must have gone back into the house.

"The sheep? They are mostly for wool, but we do eat them occasionally," he said. "Why? Are you going to argue about it?"

"Just curious."

"I'm going to visit my father. Do you want to come inside?"

"That depends. Is your family going to want me to eat a

little baby lamb? And, on a scale of one to ten, how rude am I to turn it down?"

"About an eight. But why do you care about offending these people you'll never see again?"

I shrugged. But really I was thinking, *I like you, dummy! I don't wanna piss your family off.* He's right, though. This whole thing with him is futile, but I want it, nevertheless. A week, an hour. Whatever time with him I can get.

"Come on. I'll make sure they know you don't eat little baby lambs."

It was barely sprinkling then, so I gave him his raincoat back. We stood there for a second in the doorway of the barn. It's weird, isn't it? I think of Óskar as this classy European guy —way more cultured than me—but really he's a little farm boy from the south. That's precious.

"Everything go okay with your brother?"

"I told him I want to put Pabbi in a home. I know it's wrong, that I should have more respect for the man who raised me, but that person is gone most of the time. I want Bryndis to be safe, and I want to come home."

I could relate. To all of it, in a weird way. "What'd Karl say?"

"That we'd talk about it. For now, he's giving me the keys to Mamma's summer home. Little place just off the water in the Westfjords. No electricity, but there is hot water and a gas stove. I will survive there until winter comes."

He also said that Björk has arrangements to stay with a friend. Apparently, these when-Óskar-finally-gets-the-balls-to-ditch-Jack plans have been in place for a long time.

When we went into the house, Óskar went into the living room and his dad gave him an even bigger bear hug than Karl had. Bryndís showed up and pulled me into the kitchen. "Let's give them some time alone."

Bryndís made some coffee, and she, Karl, and I sat at the kitchen table and chatted. Both of them are really cool. Karl's a computer nerd who kinda got tossed into taking over the farm after their dad started to go downhill. Bryndís is the animal lover, though. After she finishes school, she wants to take Karl's place, and he'll go back to developing software.

Karl's been to the US before for work. To Missouri, even. He said he likes the barbecue in Kansas City. I said I'd never been there, but that there are three famous barbecue places where I live. "One of them's really old. It was founded in the forties, I think."

Of course, they laughed at me because there's a ton of older shit in Iceland than that.

Every once in a while we'd hear animated voices or roaring laughter coming from the living room. I guess when Óskar and his dad get along, they really get along.

Eventually, Óskar and the old man joined us in the kitchen, and we ended up playing poker, which, of course, I suck at. And I guess Óskar's dad was giving me shit about it, because he'd occasionally grin and grumble at me in Icelandic, then all his kids would laugh. Stonefaced Óskar won practically every round we played.

At dinnertime, Karl ordered some pizzas, and Óskar and I drove to the little town nearby to pick them up. On the way there, I thanked Óskar for stealthily demanding that one of the pizzas be plain cheese. It's so stupid, but I liked having him look out for me like that. I sat with the hot pizza boxes burning my thighs and Óskar's hand in mine again the whole way back.

Óskar's dad went to bed pretty soon after dinner and then the rest of us watched Icelandic sitcoms on TV. Óskar asked if I minded staying the night there. He said I could sleep in his old bedroom and he'd sleep on the couch. And we argued about that for a while, because I was fine with the couch, but he insisted I take the bed. What actually happened, though, is that after everyone else was asleep, Óskar snuck upstairs and curled up with me in his creaky old twin-size bed.

"I want to leave early tomorrow," he whispered. "Before Pabbi wakes up."

"Okay." I couldn't quite breathe because I was still adjusting to the fact that he was next to me, pressed up against me, just in his pajama pants and no shirt.

"Your tent is shit," he said. "It leaked on me all last night."

"Sorry. But you are the one who picked it out."

"Let's go back to Reykjavik tomorrow. I'll see about a

refund and then we will drive to the Westfjords, maybe? See that little cabin of mine?"

I have to say, I was completely unprepared for the hand that slipped down the front of my boxers. I mean, I'd figured if something like that were to happen, I'd at least get a kiss first. Call me old-fashioned . . .

"Yes. Definitely. I would love to see your cabin," I squeaked.

"Shhh." He stroked me for a second, then pulled his hand back. "Sorry. We can't do this here. But I had an overwhelming urge to know what you felt like."

Of course we couldn't screw around like that in his tiny, squishy bed with his little sister on the other side of the wall. But that didn't mean I wasn't having a few overwhelming urges of my own.

I rolled forward, shifting my weight on top of him. I growled, "Fine. Go back to your couch. But I want a goodnight kiss first."

He was tense at first; we both were. I got lost somewhere between trying to be all sexy and commanding or, like, playful. I grabbed a fistful of his hair with one hand and gently trailed my fingertips down his abs with the other. I'm not sure which worked, but his shoulders relaxed and mine did, too. I sank farther toward him, and—

Accidentally pushed him off the mattress. FML. He landed on his ass next to the bed and smirked at me from the floorboards. His hair was all messy, and there was a surprisingly large tent in his pajama pants. "Told you we couldn't do this."

I whimpered an apology while he whipped a bathrobe out of his closet and pulled it on.

"So sorry. How's your ass?" I whispered.

"My ass?" he said. "It is hoping you have some better moves than that."

Then he snickered and headed off to the couch downstairs. I lay on my back in his little boyhood bed and spent most of the night thinking about the impossibility of my mouth against his.

At the time, I didn't think of you, but looking back, I can't help but remember when we first kissed. Back when everything was new and sort of terrifying and intense. That intensity fades. Eventually, and with the right person, passion turns to stability. We trade lust for real love.

A leap and a swap.

I am not cut out for this. I am, despite the tattoos and sailor's vocabulary, what some would call "boyfriend material." Yes, I want sex. I definitely want sex. But I also want things beyond that. And every second I get closer to Óskar, the more I hate that I'll never be able to have with him what I once had with you.

So, that's what we talked about today. Óskar woke me up at, like, four in the morning because old Icelandic dads tend to get up way super early. We left and ate breakfast in the car, drove back to Reykjavik, where Óskar worked his customer service skills and got me a refund on the camping equipment. And then we were supposed to drive up to his cabin, but we ended up sitting in my rental car in an empty parking lot facing the sea with mountains just on the other side. And, basically, I was like, *Nope, can't do this because: feelings.* And he was like, *Yeah, I've also got that complex emotion bizness going on, but long-distance relationships are bullshit, so please decide between ending this today or next week.*

And I said today.

Then, in an empty parking lot facing the sea with mountains just on the other side, Óskar let me kiss him goodbye.

I don't know what to say about that kiss, Vivian. Just like that time with Shannon when I said there aren't words to describe how the harbor looks at night, I can't tell you about kissing Óskar. Except to say that it felt like no kiss ever should.

It hurt. Everything does.

Afterward, he pulled a black marker out of his backpack and wrote the address to his cabin on an untatted part of my left forearm. Then he got out of the car and walked away.

And so now I'm sitting in some café reliving that awful kiss. Trying to decide if I want to rent another tent. Or maybe I need a hotel and some rest.

Or, you know, a little cabin by the water.

Because these Sharpie scribbles on my arm say that Óskar didn't intend for our first kiss to be our last. And I'm not so sure I did, either.

chapter nineteen

Miles Away to Vivian Girl

June 20 10:13 AM

Hostel is such a scary word. So unwelcoming. But that's where I am right now. Or rather, I just checked out, but I'm using the Wi-Fi in the café downstairs to gather my thoughts before I leave. It wasn't exactly a horror show, but I'm not a fan of hostels, of sharing a room with three complete strangers. I had a hell of a time finding some privacy in this place, eventually sneaking into an unlocked janitor's closet last night so I could call Mom without all these random strangers overhearing my neurotic gay shit.

Mamochka answered my Skype. She was in the kitchen, dripping wet. Water-balloon-fight day. "Hi, baby!"

"Hey, Mamochka. Where's Mom?"

She frowned at me with that combination of hurt and worry —I didn't want to talk to her? I needed the shrink instead?— but she went to find Mom anyway.

Of course, Mom was all wet and grassy, too. I felt a sting

of jealousy, sudden homesickness for Camp I wasn't expecting. I miss my campers, V.

"Where are you?" She peered into the screen.

"Broom closet in a hostel," I said.

"Why are you in a broom closet in a hostel, Miles? What happened with the hotel?"

"Óskar broke up with Jack."

I was afraid she'd try to play dumb or something, but she just busted out this big smile. "Did he? That's wonderful news!"

"Mother," I said, "I need to know your professional opinion of Óskar Franz Magnússon."

"Miles," she said, imitating my tone, "you know I can't divulge patient information."

"But . . . like . . . parental advice . . . ?" I couldn't even form complete sentences. Ugh, she makes me so nervous sometimes, like everything I say is going down on the permanent psychiatric record of me that she's building in her mind. It's so much easier to talk to Mamochka.

She could tell I was getting frustrated. She told me to take a deep breath.

I did.

"Now, tell me what's going on."

"Nothing," I said. "I like him. I think *I* just broke up with him."

She looked at me like I'd just announced I joined the Fox News anchor team. "You like Óskar?"

"Wasn't that your plan? Send me somewhere nice with this super-hot guy to take my mind off of things?"

"What? No. That sounds like something your Mamochka would do. I didn't have any ulterior motives. Óskar?" She paused and shook her head. "I didn't even know you were interested in guys."

"Mom!"

"Miles!" she said again. "You haven't had a boyfriend since you were thirteen. To be honest—and you know I'd never, ever say this to anyone but you—I thought that was a phase."

"Oh my God!" A practicing psychologist who specializes in adolescent sexuality actually trying to tell me *it's just a phase.*

"I'm sorry." She said how at the time it made sense for me to try to emulate the happiness of my parents . . . or something like that. "Obviously I was wrong. You know I'm fine with it, and you don't need a label."

"Oh my God," I said again. "Yeah, Mom. I'm not thirteen and confused."

"Then what's the problem?"

"I'm eighteen and confused!"

She laughed and then I laughed. My face felt so hot.

"I REALLY like him. It's like this big stupid crush, and I hate it. And he wants me to go stay with him at this cabin, but he also said he doesn't want to do a long-distance thing, and, like, I don't know what's worse. Is it worth it to go hang out with him for ten more days and be that much more into him so that it's that much worse when I go? Or just, like, spend the next week and a half trying not to think about him and what could have been and—holy shit, I am just miserable. Like, when do I get to stop being miserable?!"

"Okay," she said. "Let me preface this by stating that I by no means want to present you with false hope—I'm saying this so you'll understand that I have been in your situation before. You know that when I met your Mamochka, she was married to someone else and living in another country."

"Yeah."

"So." She threw up her hand. "It was worth it. For me it was. I went forward understanding that it would be only a temporary thing, but I would rather have had a day with her than a lifetime of wondering what I'd missed with that pretty little Russian girl, you know? But Óskar doesn't strike me as a liar, and if he's telling you this is all you get, then you have to fully understand that risk. And it seems like you do."

"Yeah."

"You're overthinking it. I can tell. All right. Okay. This is going to embarrass both of us, but you're forcing me to say it—"

"Oh, God!"

"Go find that pretty little Icelandic man and, well, just promise me you'll use protection, okay?"

"Mom!"

"That's it. That's my professional opinion, Miles. HAVE. FUN. You can't expect to marry every person who looks up at you through their eyelashes. It's okay to be a part of someone's story and not their happy fairytale ending."

"Fuuuuuuck."

"Miles, we need to talk about something else." Her tone changed drastically, and everything in me clenched up.

"Uh?"

"I called the hospital last night, and Dr. Morris told me Vivian has pneumonia."

"Shit." Not good. Very not good. "I'm coming home."

"Son, there is nothing you can do, here or there, to help her. You can pray, and that's about it."

"Fuck that. Pray!"

"I know you're having trouble with faith, but it helps, Miles. It does. Even some scientific studies—"

"Fuck that," I said.

There's this Chinese fable that I've always liked, this theory that certain people you meet are connected to you by an invisible red thread. The two people connected by the red thread are destined to be lovers, regardless of place, time, or circumstances. This magical cord may stretch or tangle, but it can never break.

Mom told me to pray, and all I could do was picture that red thread, follow it in my mind. Across an ocean of black waves, winding halfway across the United States. I found the thread and followed it all the way back to a hospital, down the corridors of medicine smell, to a room with a body, boyish again from over a year without her hormones. I tugged at the cord, gathering up the slack and saw it feeding into the body like an IV.

Mom wanted me to pray, but all I could do was tear at our red thread. Rip it out of your arm.

Miles Away to Vivian Girl

June 21 12:45 PM

When I got to Óskar's cabin—

Yes, of course I went to Óskar's cabin. What did you expect?

He said, "What took you so long?"

And I shrugged, speechless and shy. I stood there for a moment in his doorway. Behind me, the most gorgeous scenery you can imagine. This blue, blue lake and mountains, all this green. And in front of me, the most gorgeous guy you can imagine. Blue, blue eyes and a T-shirt that fit him just a little too tight.

He reached for me, pulling me into the cabin by the waistband of my jeans.

I took a breath. I put you out of my mind.

"I baked you a cake," he said. It was a St. Louis gooey butter cake, which he was disappointed to learn I'd never had before. "Not many Missouri-specific dessert recipes to be found. But it is vegetarian."

I said I appreciated the effort.

He responded by pinching a chunk off the corner of the cake and cramming it in my mouth.

"It's really, really good," I said. I grabbed his wrist and licked his sticky fingers clean one by one. "Let's save it for later."

The cabin was pretty dirty and dusty. Óskar said his family used to go there every summer, but no one had been since his mom died five years ago. And there were cardboard boxes scattered around, Óskar's things. He told me later that he'd gone to see Jack—to have a real talk, a final one, and to get some of his stuff. He didn't tell me much about it, just that Jack was aloof and cold.

Sorry to change the subject like that. I'm in this little café and I feel weird about this, like someone's going to peek over my shoulder and see this intimate stuff. And I feel weird about you, about saying this stuff. This very vivid and alive stuff that I did with a very vivid and alive person while I'm ignoring the message on my phone.

I will say that I enjoyed it. And he enjoyed it. We enjoyed ourselves. More than once last night.

In the break between the first and the second time, Óskar brought the whole cake pan and a pair of forks and we lay in bed together and had dessert.

Gay sex, followed by cake in bed. "Óskar, I think this is the definition of hedonism. You're going to make me fat again."

"Fat again?"

"Yeah. I looked kind of different a year ago." I felt around on the floor for my pants and got my phone. Skimming through my photos, I saw your face again and again, but I swiped at them until I found a photo of only me.

"Aww. You look like Andy from *Parks and Rec*. He's thinner now, too." And then we had a brief conversation about *Jurassic*

World, and I realized—happily—that it'd probably still be at the theater when I get back home. Until that moment I hadn't been thinking about anything that might happen when I got home, not even something as mundane as sitting in the theater with Brian, trying not to get caught by the grouchy old theater manager when we put our feet up on the seats. I hadn't been thinking about the future at all, actually.

Óskar pinched me on the hip and brought me back to the present. To him. "I'm jealous. It won't be here in Iceland for many more months."

I had to bite my lip to keep myself from inviting him back with me. Shut up, Miles, shut up.

A few minutes later, Óskar put the cake aside and retrieved a tablet from his boxes in the living room. "I looked different a year ago, too."

I waited while he angled his screen away from me and flipped through his camera roll. After a moment, he laid the tablet face down on his chest. "You can't laugh. You have to understand that I'm doing the mirror selfie ironically."

"Okay. Yeah, I won't."

But he showed me the screen, and I did laugh. "Oh my God, what is this? What am I looking at?"

The boy—and let me stress the word *BOY*—in the picture was frail, stick thin, all ribs, and sunken chested. And—"You little fraud. You're a ginger."

He shrugged and plucked at a strand of platinum hair. "Björk's doing."

"Wha—How, I mean . . . ?"

"I've been changing my landscape," he said with a little laugh. "To see how Yak would react if I looked a little more . . . mature. He hates it."

"Oh." I looked at the photo again. The shirtless boy in the mirror selfie was nineteen, but he could have easily been twelve. "That dude really is a pedophile."

"Sorry to bring him up."

I reached past him and set the tablet on the nightstand next to his side of the bed. Then we curled up together. I traced my fingers over his tight little abs, buried my face in his blond locks. Óskar smelled like vanilla and Ivory soap.

He told me he hated working out, hated how his long hair got in the way, and the hassle of all the bleach.

Funny thing, isn't it? Both of us with our bodies in this state of flux. We probably look better than we have in our lives, but it just doesn't feel right. I'll go home and start eating again, gain back most of what I lost. And he'll quit exercising, cut his hair. A year from now, we'll probably look like different people all over again. Not who we were before, but a sort of hybrid formed between now and then.

A little bit later, we were all over each other again. I mean, there's not much else to do in a cabin with no Wi-Fi, no electricity.

Afterward, he said he was glad I came. And I said I was glad he came. He meant to the cabin. I did not.

I wanted to ask if I was doing okay. If he could tell I

hadn't actually done some of that stuff before. I almost spilled our secrets then, about the way you and I used to have sex. How your dysphoria sometimes sent you into a panic when I touched you or even attempted to look at you without your clothes. I loved you I loved you I loved you. I would have loved every part of you, Vivian.

I woke up this morning with my fingertips tangled in someone else's hair. A hip, warm and naked, next to mine. I kept my eyes closed and imagined it was you. It should have been you. I don't know why I'm here and you're not.

Mom told me once that she thought that when you tried to kill yourself you were just tired. You were tired, she said, and you made a mistake. Too small of a word, *mistake*. Mistakes are the sort of thing that can be fixed with a pencil eraser or an apology or something. They don't normally end in things like court dates and feeding tubes, do they?

And a girl like you—beautiful and snarky and braver than anyone I've ever met—a girl like you couldn't have ended with pneumonia, right? Stupid word. Silent *P*. It can't have happened like that.

Óskar told me how to get to this café, free Wi-Fi so I could check my phone.

There is a message, and I'm ignoring it:

Call home as soon as you get this. We love you, son.

chapter twenty

Miles Away to Vivian Girl

June 22 4:02 PM

June 21 is the summer solstice, the day when Iceland experiences twenty-four-hour sunlight, making the day you died literally the longest of my life.

I eventually called home, because I did actually need to hear someone say it. Mamochka was crying, blubbering and completely unintelligible as soon as she answered my Skype. And then Mom.

Mom was crying, too.

"Just say it."

And she did.

Then I threw my goddamn phone across the parking lot of the café. Cracked the screen all over again. And when I got back to Óskar's cabin, I put it out of its misery once and for all. Forgot it was in my pocket when I walked fully clothed into the ice-cold water next to his house.

Is it a lake or a river? The ocean? I don't even know. But it must be fed by glaciers. It was a cold I'd never experienced before.

Óskar came out the front door and followed me along the shoreline. "Little cold, isn't it?"

"She died." I couldn't speak your name to him. Yeah, he owned one of your paintings, but he'll never know you. Never meet you, even.

Óskar, smarter than me, stripped down to his underwear before wading in and dragging me out. He undressed me on the porch, because there's nobody around for miles and there's no sense dripping all over the house. Your boots were flooded, two or three cups of water poured out when he held them upside down.

I shivered in my dripping wet undies while Óskar ran a bath. We sank into the warm water together, him in front of me. His hips between my thighs.

I stared at his back. His hair was damp and curled at the ends. There was a little constellation of freckles next to his spine. On a towel rack beside the tub, he'd draped his parents' old bathrobes. They were hand-knitted by someone as skilled as Mamochka. I could only tell by the cuffs, which were stitched up with yarn instead of needles and thread, that they weren't from a factory.

Suddenly everything in the room seemed to be telling me a story. The stitches on the robes, the condensation streaming down the walls, the curved posture of Óskar's back. Suddenly I understood Óskar. I heard all the things he'd never been able to tell me out loud.

I touched his shoulder, and he flinched. He must have been off in another world. I whispered, "What happened to your mother, Óskar?"

And he answered, just as softly, "She hung herself in the barn."

"Who found her?"

"Who do you think?"

Everything made sense. In the most tragic way. I knew then why he'd always been one step ahead of me, how he was always able to predict exactly what I would need. He understood me in a way that maybe nobody else ever will.

Óskar trembled and let out one little sob. I grabbed him around the shoulders and pulled him close. I felt everything then. All at once. Sorrow and anger and hopelessness. His skin against me and my hard cock pressed against his back. I burrowed my face into his soft hair and held tight as he whimpered, but I found that I couldn't cry.

Because I always tell you my secrets, I must admit what I was feeling then. All of my emotions had come back. Everything I had—and hadn't—been feeling for the past eighteen months. All at once. It was too much. So, when one hit me harder than the rest, I decided to hold on to it. Just to get me through to the next minute. The next hour.

I fell in love with him.

I hope I can forgive myself someday. For letting it happen so soon after you were gone.

For letting it happen at all.

Much, much later into that never-ending day, we brought a couple old quilts and lay out in the yard. Gotta experience that midnight sun, right?

We drank his bottle of toolbox Brennivín.

Black Death. The irony is not lost on me.

Sandwiched between the quilts, Óskar straddled me and pulled a felt-tip pen from his pocket. "Tell me what you Americans call this."

"Uh, a Sharpie?"

"Magic Marker," he said.

"MagicK markergh," I echoed, a little drunk.

"Yes." He nodded and tugged my shirt up. I leaned up a little so he could pull it over my head. Then he drew this symbol on my chest, a stylized equilateral compass with decorative etchings along the arms.

I traced his sloppy, drunken lines with my fingertip. Right over my heart. I knew instantly what my next tattoo would be. "What is it?"

"*Vegvísir.*" According to Wikipedia: an Icelandic magical stave meant to guide the bearer through rough weather. "It helps when you are lost."

He also told me it's tradition after the solstice to roll

naked in the morning dew. I think what we did probably counts.

This morning, we went back to the café for breakfast and Wi-Fi. He borrowed some guy's phone and spent half an hour trying to find me a flight back home, while I did the same by poking around on my iPad. Nothing available for a couple of days. Tourist season, and all.

I called home, and Mom told me I didn't have to come. That maybe it'd be best for me not to be there when your parents buried you under the wrong name and in a suit.

"That awful church is coming to picket," she said. "Just stay there."

I was too fucked to disagree. I don't know if it's wrong or right for me to skip your funeral. It looks bad, I know. But I'm kind of through with caring what the rest of the world thinks.

It's hard to describe how I'm feeling now. It's funny, this impending sense of . . . calm? The threat of your death, the burden of protecting you, of failing to save you, of finding some way to honor you—before yesterday, those things were always in the back of my mind. And now sometimes my mood will twist. I'll find myself worried and worked up again, only to realize that my worst nightmares have already come true. There aren't any more dark corners for my anxieties to hide.

I feel empty, but more in a blank canvas sort of way. What'll I do with myself now? Who am I if not the guardian of your hospital tubes and all that red thread?

Miles Away to Vivian Girl

June 29 3:42 PM

Óskar asked me if I wanted to continue my loop around the Ring Road. I guess he figured it'd take my mind off of things. So we left the cabin that we'd only just settled into, got another tent, and drove. That's what I've been doing for the past six days. Sightseeing and sex. I think I fucked Óskar in every corner of Iceland.

Until it just wasn't the answer anymore.

After a while, things . . . imploded. I think it was the day we were at the glacier lagoon and I got caught up taking a million photos of the ice floating in the water, scattered on the beach. It doesn't look like ice, V. It's like glass. Little sculptures. The way the colors swirl into each other, translucent into opaque, light into dark. Of course I got preoccupied.

And Óskar got bored. After I put my camera up, I turned around, and he was gone. Empty beach. Not a soul to be found. I looked around for him forever. I started to get worried he'd somehow gotten carried off into the sea. Eventually I thought to check the car, and there he was stretched out in the back seat. Headphones on, napping away.

I woke him up and growled at him like he was somebody's toddler, but he shrugged me off. "You found me. What is the problem?"

The problem was that he didn't think it was a problem.

The problem was that losing him for twenty minutes on a barren, icy beach was just a portent of things to come. He has been my compass lately (and I'd like to think maybe I've done the same for him). Who knows if I'll get lost again the second I get home?

And the problem was that I couldn't say any of that out loud because it'd only make both of us feel like shit. So I just got in the front seat and drove.

Wrong move. I had tugged the wrong Jenga block, and the whole tower came crashing down. After that, the anger settled in, and I let it stay. I took it out on him because I thought it would help me find a way to pull myself away from him and remain intact.

I tried to make myself forget that he was struggling, too. He and Jack had been together way longer than you and I. But every time Óskar would mention his name, or try to relate, I would so cruelly snap back about how Jack wasn't dead.

I'm a monster. I'd thought things were getting better, but I've become a monster instead.

By the time our little trip was nearing its end, I hated Óskar and Óskar hated me. Furniture assembly, ha! The true test of emotional endurance is camping and car rides.

When we finally circled back around to the southern coast, Óskar requested to be dropped off at his family's home. We arrived a couple hours later. I pulled into the driveway and shut off the car.

"The, uh, flight package thing my parents bought includes a trip to the Blue Lagoon. I guess I'll be doing that tomorrow morning before my flight."

"Tourist trap," Óskar said. "But do what you must."

"Uh, well, I'll be there tomorrow, and I mean, if you wanted to—"

"Don't."

"Okay."

And then he did something he hadn't before. He reached for my hand. We sat like that for a while in complete silence. Then he grabbed his pack out of the back seat, got out of the car, and walked up to the house.

He didn't say a word. He didn't kiss me. Or even look back.

I waited, watching, until Karl answered the door and invited him in.

And, just like that, my chapter in Óskar's story was over. I got a paper cut from turning the page.

He didn't show at the Blue Lagoon this morning, of course. So I ended up alone, soaking in the milky ice-blue waters of Iceland's most romantic geothermal spa. Without his presence, though, I'm starting to feel like myself again. Dorky and self-conscious, but, yeah . . . me. When I was wading through a shallow part of the lagoon, I spotted a pretty girl, and we grinned at each other. Then I hit a ridge across the uneven bottom and fell face first into the water, spilling my drink. Yep.

And now I'm in that great glass airport, soaking up my last few moments in this place. Some idiotic part of me can't help but stare at the gates and imagine a boy with a backpack and a bun crashing through into my arms.

Not gonna happen, but I have a few more minutes to pretend.

Miles Away to Vivian Girl

June 29 9:03 PM

I time-traveled today, gaining back the six hours I lost at the beginning of my trip. I think Mamochka was supposed to pick me up at the airport in St. Louis, but my best friend was there instead.

"'Sup?" Brian said, leaning on a pillar, giving me the guy nod.

"Oh, don't fucking do that," I said, throwing up my arms. "Gimme a hug."

He hugged me, and dwarfed me, all six and a half feet of him. I thought of Óskar, how he must've felt standing next to me. And then I imagined Óskar and Brian trying to carry on a conversation. A stepladder would have to be involved.

When we got out of the noisy gate, he asked me about the trip.

"It was . . . I mean, I . . . you know . . ." I said. "Not sure about the words . . ." Already I was back to being my usual introverted self. Not the guy who blurts out his life story to strangers anymore.

He laughed. "Oh yeah, forgot who I was talking to for a minute there. Okay, Miles, tell me one thing about your trip."

"One thing?" I raised an eyebrow and tried to figure out how to sum my Icelandic experience up into one act that a bro from Missouri would appreciate. "Well, I made out with Björk."

"Hell yeah."

Then it was time to talk about you. He said since we were in the city, he could take me to the cemetery.

"I'm not ready to do that."

"Yeah." He nodded. "But let's just do it like a Band-Aid, right? Real quick."

"No."

"Damn it, Miles, I told Mamochka I'd take you. I'm tryna score points with your hot mom here, okay?"

I smiled because that felt normal, Brian and his schoolboy crush on my mama.

I tried not to think about the specifics of the situation. Of you and of death. It was easier to consider it as a favor for Mamochka, an errand. Just a quick trip to a graveyard, right? Like he said, quick like a Band-Aid.

The Missouri heat and humidity struck me in the face as soon as we left the terminal. I stripped off my hoodie and stopped to toss it in my suitcase.

Brian studied my new clothes, shaking his head. "I thought we agreed never to become hipsters, man."

"Oh shit." I started patting my pockets like I'd lost something. For a second there, Brian looked genuinely concerned. "Where did I leave my mustache? My pipe! Oh, wait . . ." I reached into my shirt pocket and pulled out the old one-finger salute. Brian cackled at me.

That felt normal, too.

It's a nice place, your cemetery. A pretty swell place to be dead. Gates and trees and whatnot. Thinking back on it, it's not the sights that I remember so much as the sounds. The buzz and drone of the cicadas. A lawn mower nearby. And beyond that, traffic sounds and city.

I didn't cry, like I thought I would. I knelt at your grave, this mound of freshly dug brown earth. I traced the letters of your name—the wrong name—with my fingertip. That's all I could think about, how thoroughly fucked it is for what's left of you to spend eternity captioned incorrectly.

It's fucked, but I'm not angry. I can't hate it, or myself, anymore. What's done is done.

So, there I was, having this intense internal monologue, when I heard a sniffle from behind me. I thought that was weird, because obviously Brian was never your biggest fan. I looked over my shoulder to tease him a little, but . . .

The sniffler wasn't Brian.

And then they rushed me. My Camp kids! My moms, too! Arms everywhere, a gigantic rolling hug in the graveyard dirt. The campers should've gone home yesterday—I hadn't thought I'd see them at all! But Mom and Mamochka rented a couple of vans and took them up to St. Louis to see Vivian's grave.

And every single one of them had on red shoes. Cheap canvas shoes decorated with spray paint, glitter glue, red fabric paint. The hashtag lives on. And, in a way, so will you.

That's when my tears started. They don't hate me after all. They aren't mad. Sure, there probably always will be people like Frankie who think I did you wrong, but the people who loved me before still love me now. They don't blame me for your headstone bearing the wrong name.

Oh, wow. Wow. That's how simple it was, to turn something so horrible, a visit to your grave, into the sweetest homecoming of my life.

Miles Away to Vivian Girl
June 30 4:32 PM

I can smell my house. I know that's a weird thing to say, but it's true. It's like when you go to a friend's house and it smells like THEIR house, then you go home and try to smell your own house, but you can't. Well, I am home, and I can smell my own house. It's difficult to describe, this mythical smell. It reminds me of when I was little and I'd sniff all the silk flowers at the craft store downtown. They don't have scents, but I sure thought they did. Mamochka would kneel down beside me and play along. She liked the tulips, and I liked the tiger lilies.

The other thing that's strange is that I have too much stuff. After living out of a suitcase for a month, all my belongings seem extraneous. Like . . . why the hell do I still have that clay teapot I made in fifth grade? It's a shitty-ass teapot, man.

God, now I'm thinking about electrrrreK Kayh-tuls.

But, anyway . . . some of this stuff is yours. I think

Mamochka is friends with a lady who runs a clothing swap for trans kids, so maybe it'll be okay for me to donate to that. I'll keep some of your favorites to give to the kids at Camp.

There are things that I need to keep and things to let go of, as well. I'm only beginning to sort that all out.

Speaking of clothes, a few hours ago, Mamochka offered to do my laundry, so I just dumped the contents of my suitcase into my laundry basket and let her have at it. She came back with the clean stuff a little bit ago and was like, "You'll have to explain these things to me sometime."

She had my bloodstained Tourist T-shirt in one hand, and a pair of obviously-not-mine teeny-tiny men's briefs in the other.

They were bright red. And so was I, I'm sure.

I swiped them from her and stuffed them underneath my pile of clean clothes. "Uh, maybe sometime."

Somewhere down the hall, I heard Mom chuckling at my expense.

It's really weird having a secret with Mom. I'm pretty sure that Mamochka has no clue what went down with me in Iceland, but Mom had her own private line. I wonder if he's called her since I've been home. I wonder if he'll keep seeing her now that he doesn't have a hotel to trade anymore. Does he even need to?

She helped him, you know? Like, he had a problem, then she offered up some tools and helped him make a plan. He did all that, and it worked. I'm practically a stranger to him, but even I could see that it worked. Sure, it's going to be shitty and painful for a while, but he's resilient, right? I can think about him, picture him a year from now, and he'll be just fine.

And in some ways, what he had to go through was even more difficult than my shit with you. He lost his mom. His dad basically forgot about him. He couldn't even live in his own home. All he had left was Jack and now he's gone too.

Yet, as scary at it seems, I envy that tangibility. I'm tired of shouting into the void and hearing only myself echoing back.

Shit. I don't know if I can do this anymore, V.

Miles Away to Vivian Girl
July 3 7:14 PM

I got another tattoo today.

Marlee was working in the shop by herself, and when I came in, she dropped the magazine she was reading and flung her arms around my neck.

"My God, where have you been?"

I said, "Iceland," but I'm pretty sure she thought I was joking.

And then she asked where you were.

I got all quiet, trying to hold it together.

I mean . . . how could she not know?

"Hey, man, shit happens," she said before I could gather my thoughts. "You're too cute for her, anyhow. Let's get you some ink."

I now have the *vegvísir* permanently on my chest. White ink. It looks like scar tissue.

Miles Away to Vivian Girl
July 4 7:32 PM

I'm glad that it's over. I think I can say that to you now. And I'm glad, too, that ending your life by turning off the ventilators was never a choice I had to make.

I went to Mom's office yesterday. While she was busy with patients, I went into the office and made paperclip chains and listened to her secretary answer the phone. Then when her last session for the day was over, I strolled down the hall and plopped my ass down on her proverbial couch.

"Hi," I said.

"Hi, Miles." She dug into one of her desk drawers and pulled out a couple granola bars. I snatched mine out of the air as she tossed it to me.

I pulled at the flap, tearing the wrapper along the seam. "I was mad at you. For the longest time, I thought it was your fault. Because you're a therapist. I thought you should have seen it coming. I thought you should have been able to stop her somehow."

"I know. I blamed myself, too," she said. "I am so sorry."

"No, I don't want you to apologize. I'm not mad anymore. It isn't your fault. Or mine, even. I just wanted to tell you," I said. "Because you're alive, and I should be talking to you. It's probably more beneficial than talking to a dead person, right?

That's what I have been doing. I've been writing to Vivian, and that's a little . . . you know? I mean, I'm sorry. I should have told you about this sooner, but I figured you'd make me stop, and I wasn't ready yet."

"Why do you think I'd make you stop?" Typical therapist question.

I peeled the wrapper back from the bar and spread it out across my knees. I attacked the bare rectangle of granola, pulling out the chocolaty bits first. "Because it's fucking crazy."

"Did it make you feel better?"

"It made me feel like I still exist."

There was a long pause. I was staring down at the mess of oats and chocolate in my lap. When I looked up, I saw that Mom was picking hers apart the same way. And she was crying.

"I'm so screwed up I made the therapist cry," I said, passing over her own box of tissues.

She wiped her eyes and got that intimidating Mom look for a second, then it left and her face softened. "You're not. You're not screwed up. Out of all of this, you were the only one who had any sense. She was just so special. She was so hard to lose. Even her parents understood that. But we were all way out of line. I never should have tried to make Vivian's situation about anyone other than her."

I'm pausing here because I want you to understand, wherever you are, that Mom is sorry. And I am sorry. And your parents might even be sorry.

We loved you.

I'm not mad at Mom anymore. She went on to say some other stuff, stuff about me and her, but I'm not sure if that's pertinent here. Like a lot of things in my life, I have yet to figure out if these messages are for me or for you. I know what they started out as. Now I'm not so sure.

I guess they have to be about me now. Because I am the only one left.

Mom told me that writing unseen letters like this is totally sane and, actually, something she recommends that some of her patients try. But I've decided to stop

and

just

live

my

life.

It's like the megapixels. I'm doing the same thing, here, aren't I? Trying to compress all that's happened into data. Everything's zeros and ones.

I am not a photograph. I am not binary code.

At the end of all this, I am still as confused as ever about the almighty Purpose of My Trip. But with all that happened, good and bad, it served as indisputable proof that whether I'm bleeding in the mud or wrapped in someone else's arms, I have no choice but to continue on. My synapses are still firing, and my heart is still pounding in my chest.

I still exist.

I am here now at your grave. There's dirt and grass and gates and trees. It's dusk, and the fireflies are twinkling, but I'm not really getting any of that because I'm staring into a screen. In a moment, though, I'll hit send. Tuck my new phone into my pocket and look up. There will be fireflies and a sunset. Trees and grass.

And fireworks. There'll be fireworks because it's my Independence Day.

I'll dig my fingers into the dirt covering your casket, and I'll wish, for at least a moment, that my fingers were winding into your curly hair.

And then I'll let go.

I'll get up from where I'm sitting and step out of your boots. Your oxblood Doc Martens with the dent on the toe. Your boots, V. Your fucking boots.

I'll peel off my socks and walk barefoot away from your burial plot. I'll walk slowly, careful not to step on some fucking hypodermic needle or something. Or a bumblebee.

And I'll be walking. Away.

And, yeah, I'll probably cry. But I'll be smiling too. I mean it this time, Vivian. This is my last message to you.

epilogue

Óskar Franz Magnússon to Miles Away

December 12 7:32 AM

Halló, American boy.

acknowledgments

Thank you to my besties Keenan Pixley, Laura McElroy, and Aleshia Morley for being my first readers and convincing me I should keep on doing this writing thing. All the love to Mom, Dad, Josh, and all my extended family for molding me into the strange, artsy creature I am today. Thank you to Travis Rutledge for taking me to Iceland and then allowing me to basically ignore you for a few years while I figured out how to write this book. You have my heart forever.

Thank you to my CPs: Laura Creedle, Dannie Morin, Laura Hitchcock, Laura Felicetti, Jennifer Todhunter, Maria Dascalu, Ryan Page, Lena Maye, Polly J. Brown, and Sera Flynn. And to TC Safavi for dropping us all off at the Kiddie Pool. Big, big thanks to Jessica Gibson and Meredith Russo for all your help with Vivian.

Thank you Francesca Lia Block and all the magical faerie girls I met through your workshop, especially Jessa Marie Mendez, Jilly Dreadful, Laura Thorne, Melanie Terrill, Jess Mullen, Jennifer Martin, and Tegan Webb. You're my oldest and truest writer buddies. I'll always cherish our late-night word wars, tarot sessions, and ridiculous inside jokes. You people get me.

Thank you to #TeamMoe, especially Sophie Gonzales, who single-handedly got me through six months of sub hell by being hilarious and snarky and awake on the other side of the planet so I could have someone to complain to at three a.m. I can't wait to see your books on the shelf someday soon.

Thank you to all the magic-makers who turned my scribbles into something real. Alana Saltz, you are the guardian angel of this book. I'll be forever grateful that you picked my story out of the slush and gave me the courage to submit it to agents. Thank you to Moe Ferrara for being the world's coolest agent. Your editorial notes are always full of win and I really appreciate all the care and attention you have given me and Miles. Thank you to Jim Secula and everyone at HMH who worked to make this book beautiful inside and out. Thanks to my cover designer, Sharismar Rodriguez. I can't get over how stunning this cover is. And, lastly, thank you to my editor Margaret Raymo for giving this offbeat little tale a home. I thought editing would be frustrating and terrifying, but I haven't felt overwhelmed even once. Thank you for making my wildest dream come true.

RESOURCES:

If you're having suicidal thoughts, please, please reach out to someone. I promise you that you're not alone and there are people who can help.
Trans Life Line can be reached at 1-877-565-8860.
The Trevor Project has a 24/7 lifeline at 1-866-488-7386 or you can text "Trevor" to 1-202-304-1200.
The National Suicide Prevention Hotline is 1-800-273-8255.